BLACK FROG

B. D. SMITH

Black Rose Writing | Texas

Second printing / First Hardcover printing

This is a work of fiction. Names, characters, businesses, places, events, and incidents are either the products of the author's imagination or used in a fictitious manner. Any resemblance to actual persons, living or dead, or actual events is purely coincidental.

ISBN: 978-1-68433-282-3 (Paperback); 978-1-944715-92-2 (Hardcover)
PUBLISHED BY BLACK ROSE WRITING
www.blackrosewriting.com

Printed in the United States of America
Suggested Retail Price (SRP) $18.95 (Paperback); $23.95 (Hardcover)

Black Frog is printed in Candara

For Mindy
The love of my life

BLACK FROG

PROLOGUE

It was late spring, a few hours after sunset, and a full moon was high over the vast northern forests. Peter slipped out of his barracks building and quickly moved toward the perimeter fence of the prisoner of war camp. The camp had not been open long when he first arrived about a year ago, and the guards - all local men, were new on the job then and always alert. But that had gradually changed, and Peter knew that the guard manning the tower he was approaching was probably already asleep.

The POWs didn't have it easy. The hours were long and the work was demanding – felling, trimming, and hauling timber through the long brutal winters and working in potato fields in the warmer months. But the Geneva Convention was followed for the most part, Red Cross inspections were routine, and the prisoners were generally not mistreated. The barracks were cramped and poorly heated by wood stoves, however, and the potato-heavy diet and grinding routine of hard manual labor took its toll. The anticipated end of the war was on everyone's mind.

Escape attempts were not uncommon in the POW camps located farther south in more populated areas, but here there had only been a handful. It was not so much the guards that discouraged escapes at this northern forest camp as it was the surrounding wilderness that stretched away in every direction. Others had attempted escape before Peter, but rather than trying to break out of the camp itself, with its guard towers, barbed wire fences, and bright lights, they had simply walked away from their work crews in the forest.

These walk-offs often seemed to occur on the spur of the moment, with little planning and little thought given to how to survive and where to go. Most of the POWs were city boys with no experience surviving in the wilderness. Peter suspected that the guards might actually have looked the other way in anticipation of a break in the tedium and a few days of entertainment tracking the runaways. None of the POWs had remained at large for long. Their absence was quickly noted at the mid-day or evening head counts and they were routinely recaptured. Tracking them through the snow was easy in the winter, and during the warmer months escaped prisoners were often relieved to be caught, preferring the solitary confinement they could expect to the clouds of biting insects they encountered in the endless expanse of forest.

Peter, however, was no city boy. He had grown up on a remote northern farm and was used to hard manual labor, long winters, and the swarms of insects that summer brought. Like most of his childhood friends Peter was also an avid hunter and trapper, and his knowledge of wilderness survival skills had earned him a coveted award from one of the local youth groups he had belonged to as a teen. The award, a silver disc about the size of a fifty-cent piece, had his initials engraved on one side and an embossed lightning bolt on the other – the symbol of the youth group. He had carried this talisman with him throughout the war and managed to hold on to it even after he was wounded and captured during the early days of the Battle of Normandy.

Peter slipped silently under the lowest strand of wire, and as he walked confidently toward the dark forest shadows, out of the glare of the bright prison lights, he rubbed the lightning bolt award for good luck.

Unlike the previous "walk-off" escapees, Peter had been planning for months. Hiding his fluency in the guttural language of his captors, he listened in on their conversations whenever the opportunity arose. At first the thick regional dialect and slang of the rural woodsmen who manned the guard towers and oversaw the lumbering crews was difficult to understand, but he slowly picked it up, and learned a lot. Albert, one of the friendlier work crew overseers, was a particularly valuable source of information, and would often talk with other guards about his frequent hunting trips in the local area.

It was from listening in on one of Albert's conversations that Peter learned that his best chance for escape lay to the northeast of the camp, where a lumbering road and canoe portage trails converged on a small community on the banks of a major river. He wasn't sure how many miles he would have to travel through the forest before hitting the portage trail, but thought he had a good chance of reaching the river in just a few days. Peter's plan was to then pass himself off as a local and gain passage on a boat heading down to the coast. There he could try to contact sympathizers who might be able to smuggle him out to safety.

And instead of walking away from a work crew, Peter decided to escape from the camp itself. If he could slip past the guard tower and under the barbed wire perimeter fence of the camp soon after lights out, he would have a good ten-hour head start before they discovered him missing at the morning head count.

It was a good plan, he thought, and if it failed he would just wait out the war in the camp. The food was marginal at best – heavy on starch, and the day-to-day existence was not easy – with long cold winters and hard manual labor. But he was healthy, and his leg, broken when he was captured, did not bother him much anymore. Navigating the rocky terrain of the forest floor at night would be hazardous, but he hoped that the full moon would help him to avoid falling and perhaps reinjuring his leg.

Peter also was well equipped for a several days march through the dark forest. His small knapsack contained several baked potatoes and some heels of bread, along with a length of rusty window screen he had salvaged from an abandoned cabin a few months back and fashioned into a head net to protect him from the swarms of insects. He also had picked up a heavy flannel shirt that a guard had dropped on one of their work details, which he would put on before passing himself off as a local. And his prize possession, critical for his escape plan, was a crude compass he had fashioned out of a sewing needle, a magnetized electrical coil, and the tin top from a can of peaches.

Peter paused fifty yards or so into the forest and turned to make sure that his escape had not been noticed. He then walked over to a small clearing where a tree fall had created an opening in the forest canopy and moonlight illuminated a small patch of delicate white lady slipper wild orchids. Smiling to himself and breathing in the crisp night air that carried the smell of tamaracks, Peter consulted his crude compass and then headed off toward the northeast.

He made good progress through the forest for the first few hours, crossing several small streams and skirting a small beaver pond, but then the terrain became more difficult, with large rocks slippery with moss and the ground covered with a constant tangle of tree roots. Peter stopped about three in the morning at the base of a steep escarpment and tried to rest for several hours, but his leg had begun to ache, and a thick cloud of insects swarmed around his makeshift head net, making sleep impossible.

With first light he walked along the base of the escarpment for several miles before finding a cleft and a way up its side. It was not too difficult a climb, but about halfway up a loose rock gave way beneath him and he fell hard on his bad leg, crying out with pain in the still morning air. He continued climbing after a few minutes, but his leg now pulsed with a dull and persistent ache. Progress was difficult after that, but by mid-morning he had found the canoe portage trail angling off toward the northeast, and even with frequent stops he was able to make reasonably good time. An abandoned campsite several miles up the trail yielded a valuable surprise – someone had left a well-worn canoe paddle behind, which would serve as an excellent prop supporting Peter's claim to be a local looking for passage downriver to the coast. Using the canoe paddle as a crutch he continued along the trail and began to craft a more detailed cover story. He knew from Albert's stories that the southern terminus of the canoe portage trail was at the north end of a large lake. He could say that his canoe had been swamped in a storm and he had lost all his belongings except for the paddle, and was looking for passage down to the coast. It was a flimsy story, easily exposed, but it might work.

By mid-afternoon several other trails had joined the one he was on, and it was now wider and seemed well traveled. Soon Peter thought he could smell wood smoke and hear the faint thudding of axes against tree trunks. As he reached the crest of the next rise in the trail the smoke from a settlement could be seen above the trees, and sunlight sparkled on the swift flowing river just beyond it. He had reached his destination. Now he would have to find a way downriver.

Hearing a sound off to his left, Peter turned to see several men step out of the woods and approach him, one of them pointing a double-barreled shotgun in his general direction. He hailed them and was about to explain how he had lost his canoe and supplies when he recognized the man with the shotgun. It was Albert, the talkative guard from the prison camp. Peter's shoulders slumped and he realized he would soon be back at camp and facing a month or two in solitary confinement.

Albert gazed at him for a moment and then laughed.

"Thought you were pretty smart didn't you? Listening in on our talk. Thought I didn't know you could understand us. I saw you steal the shirt and the window screen. I've been watching you for a long time now. Sneaking around with your big ears. Soaking up all the information I was feeding you - which direction to take, how far it was to the river settlement, and the escape route downriver. Took you longer than I thought it would to get here. We've been waiting all day. But you're here now, right where I want you. You think you're going back to camp don't you? But you're not. You're finished. As soon as I found out you were in the Battle of Normandy, captured in the Bocage campaign, I started planning your escape for you, so you could end up right here. You bastards killed my baby brother in Normandy, and today I can even up the score."

Peter dropped the canoe paddle and raised his hands above his head. He hadn't understood all of what Albert had said, but there was no mistaking the prison guard's intent as he shouldered the shotgun.

1.
DOUGLAS
SATURDAY

Doug Bateman had made the trip up Route 6 to Greenville Maine from his home on the north shore of Sebec Lake countless times, and it usually took him a little over an hour. An early morning fog had slowed him considerably today, however, and he was relieved when it began to clear as he passed the Finnish Farmers Dance Hall just north of Monson. In a few miles he would be entering a stretch of road where large yellow signs warned drivers of frequent moose crossings, and the last thing he wanted was an adult moose suddenly appearing out of the fog in front of his Jeep Cherokee. Doug had been a Maine State Police trooper for more than a decade before being promoted to detective and he had seen too many examples of what a moose could do to a car and its occupants. The long spindly legs of an adult moose raised its body up above the hood of most vehicles, and seatbelts and airbags didn't help much when a thousand-pound carcass came through the windshield.

Doug crested the final hill coming into Greenville at the Indian Hill Trading Post and pulled over in front of the old McDonald's to take in the stunning view of Moosehead Lake that stretched out in front of him. In the mid-1800s Henry David Thoreau had likened the lake to "a gleaming silver platter at the end of the table," and it had seen relatively little change in the past century and a half. Forty miles long north to south and ten miles wide, the lake has a rugged and largely undeveloped coastline. Thoreau's "table" - the continuous and uninterrupted forest that stretches away to the north of Moosehead, remains one of the largest unbroken expanses of wilderness in the country. Dominated by spruce, pine, and fir, this forest zone of northern Maine, when viewed at night from space, stands out as a vast island of darkness.

Doug pulled into the parking lot of the Maine Guide Fly Shop in Greenville just as his friend Jim Hancock stepped out the front door, holding up a small bag of what Doug knew would be a selection of new flies. Jim was tall and athletic, with an easy smile, prematurely gray hair, and a fashion model's good looks. He and Doug had been friends since their undergraduate days at the University of Maine. Jim had gone on to study environmental law after graduation, and for the past decade he had been general counsel for The Maine Forest Alliance, an environmental group in Portland dedicated to protecting wilderness areas in the state. Over the years Doug and Jim had remained friends and went fishing together two or three times every summer. They always met here at the fly shop and often would just drive the short distance up along the west side of Moosehead Lake to the east outlet of the Kennebec River, which offered some of the best wild trout fishing in the country. Leaving Jim's car at the fly shop, they continued through Greenville, and as Doug turned left at the light and drove west through town, past the Kamp Kamp store and the Black Frog restaurant, Jim opened the bag on his lap, showing Doug his new flies.

"Dan and Penny have some great new Copper Johns and some Caddis larvae just in, and they say the fishing has been great this last week, with stream flow well below 2000."

Doug usually stuck with a few tried and true flies, mostly Shufelt Specials, created by the local fishing legend, Bobby Shufelt of Greenville. Jim, on the other hand, was always trying out new flies and would frequently switch to something different if the fish didn't seem interested. He was always teasing Doug for his lack of interest in trying new things – saying it was the result of him spending his entire life, except for college, in Piscataquis County, Maine, which had a population density of four people per square mile.

"Guess I'll stick with the Shufelts," Doug responded, eliciting a snort of disdain from Jim.

"Let's work the north side from the bridge downstream to the Beach Pool," Jim suggested. "It's eight now, we can pocket pick till eleven or so and then have lunch before I have to go to the town hall meeting over at the high school. You should come with me Doug. It's on the Lily Bay development plan and could easily turn nasty. We might need a state police presence."

There was only a single pickup truck in the parking lot just north of the Highway 6 Bridge over the Kennebec when they arrived, and they had the river pretty much to themselves. For the next three hours they slowly worked their way downstream in the fast, boulder-filled river, looking for the small pockets of calm water that trout favored that were located just downstream from rocks and logs. It was a beautiful day, with the sun sparkling off the water, and only a few other anglers in sight. The morning passed quickly, with Doug catching a single reasonably sized brook trout while Jim had better luck with his new Copper Johns, landing three trout and a juvenile salmon, all of which he released.

Breaking for lunch, they drove down to Kelly's Landing at Greenville Junction and sat out on the deck. Over a pitcher of cold beer and burgers they watched seaplanes taxi and take off out of West Cove and talked about the town hall meeting that afternoon, called to discuss the massive Lily Bay development project recently proposed for the east side of Moosehead Lake. The Maine Forest Alliance, along with a wide range of other environmental groups, had been opposing such development projects across Maine for more than thirty years, and Jim had become a forceful and impassioned figure in their ongoing efforts to protect Maine forests.

"It's a battle for the soul of Maine, Doug, for our way of life, and ground zero right now is right here at Moosehead Lake. More than 90 percent of Maine is forested and 95 percent of our forestlands are privately owned. Logging and harvesting of wood products have been the economic engine of Maine for more than 200 years, and you could say the forests have managed to survive despite our best efforts to eradicate them. They endured the rapacious clear-cutting and resultant massive forest fires and insect plagues of the 18th and 19th centuries, and have survived the four decades of industrial management by large forest product companies following WWII. But now they face the even greater threat of human sprawl and development."

Pausing to drain his beer and refill his glass, Jim continued his impassioned history lesson on Maine's forests.

"Changes in tax laws and world markets in the 1990s forced many of the large timber corporations like Georgia Pacific and International Paper to start selling off their holdings in smaller parcels to timber and real estate investment companies. These investment companies - TIMOs and REITs, as they're called, have a very different business model than the vertically integrated 'forest to mill' timber goliaths. The TIMOS and REITS focus on maximizing returns on shorter time horizons, and whenever it's feasible, once they exhaust the timbering potential of their holdings, they look to turn their forestlands into lucrative commercial and residential developments."

Doug had grown up hearing heated arguments from Mainers on both sides of this long unfolding struggle over who would control its forests. On one side stood the environmental groups that wanted them protected and held in the public interest, with greater controls on recreational access, timber harvesting and commercial development. Opposing them were business interests who saw the vast untapped potential of Maine's forestlands. They were often joined by Mainers in the local communities who had both relied on the forests for their livelihood for many generations and had long enjoyed largely open access to them for hunting, fishing, and exploring in snowmobiles and ATVs.

Doug knew Jim was almost finished with his monologue, so he leaned back in his chair and motioned to the waitress for the check as Jim continued.

"Southern and central Maine, the more populated regions of the state, have witnessed the most dramatic loss of forest to this expanding sprawl over the past two decades, but there has also been a surge in development along the ever-expanding northern margins of development as the TIMOs and REITS are looking for opportunities to clear forestland for planned subdivisions of vacation homes. That's what's going on right now at Moosehead – The Lily Bay development would be a huge vacation home subdivision and golf course complex on Moosehead Lake, at the edge of the largest contiguous block of undeveloped forest east of the Mississippi."

Smiling at his friend's heartfelt speech, Doug teasingly broke in.

"So where's the opposition coming from to efforts to bring progress to Piscataquis County, other than the usual suspects – the Sierra Club and other big outside environmental meddlers and tree huggers??"

Jim paused, took another sip of beer, and replied.

"Actually it's pretty interesting. When the big timber companies started selling off smaller land parcels back in the nineties, a lot of small, local environmental groups - timber trusts and conservation groups, became active in buying up and preserving forestlands. At the same time, lots of communities are looking to tourism as the economic future of central and northern Maine. So the battle lines are now forming at the local as well as the regional and national level, with lots of grassroots efforts all across the state."

Doug thought about this, and what it meant for the small towns and dispersed communities of Piscataquis County.

"Sounds like a recipe for driving a wedge between friends and neighbors, Jim– it could tear communities apart on a very personal level."

Jim grimaced.

"That's why you need to come with me to the town hall meeting on the planned Lily Bay development, Doug – see for yourself the firestorm that's coming."

They drove back downtown so Jim could pick up his car, and as

Doug followed him into the high school parking lot and pulled in next to his friend's shiny red BMW, he was surprised to see that the lot was almost full. The BMW certainly stood out against the other vehicles in the lot, Doug thought, and sent exactly the wrong message – here's an affluent outsider from the big city coming to town to tell us what's best for us, and what's best for the forests. Opening the back of his 1987 Jeep Cherokee, Doug unlocked a large steel storage box that was bolted to the frame. Reaching in he extracted his Heckler & Koch HK45 LEM .45 service pistol and slipped the holster onto his belt. Grabbing his lightweight windbreaker from the back seat that had "STATE POLICE" in bright yellow on the back, Doug joined Jim and they walked across the gravel parking lot toward the main entrance of the high school.

Doug wondered if the Piscataquis County Sheriff's Office would have sent anyone up from Dover-Foxcroft, the county seat, to cover the event, and his question was answered as he noticed Anne Quinn's dark green mid-70s Toyota Land Cruiser parked close to the high school entrance. Anne was an investigator with the sheriff's office and she and Doug had worked together on a high profile serial killer case a few years back. He hadn't seen her in a while but had heard that Charlie Hudson, the new Piscataquis County Sheriff, had been giving her a hard time since his election the previous fall. Apparently Anne's status as something of a local hero for her role in their murder case of a few years ago did not sit well with Hudson. He had been targeting her with critical comments and menial assignments ever since becoming sheriff, so Doug was not surprised that Anne had been sent up to Greenville to do crowd control on a weekend.

He thought she would probably be scanning the crowd that filed into the high school auditorium for potential troublemakers, and as he and Jim stepped through the front doors he saw Anne leaning against a line of lockers. She was watching the crowd and talking to Jim Torben. Doug was surprised to see Torben at the town hall, since he had recently been promoted to Chief Deputy in the Piscataquis

County Sherriff's Office, and normally wouldn't be expected to be working this kind of weekend duty. He wondered if Hudson had sent Torben to keep an eye on Anne and report back, or if Torben had decided on his own to keep Anne company. Jim and his wife June were good friends with Anne, and prior to his promotion he had often managed to get himself assigned to team up with her. Jim had just said something to make Anne laugh, and her bright smile flashed briefly before vanishing as she saw Doug. Frowning, she walked over to Doug.

"What brings the state police to Greenville, Detective Bateman?"

Hiding his surprise at her cold greeting, Doug smiled and introduced Jim.

"Jim Hancock and I were just over fishing the east outlet and stopped by to catch the town hall meeting. Jim, this is Investigator Anne Quinn and Deputy Chief Jim Torben with the county sheriff's office. Jim is with the Maine Forest Alliance."

Shaking Anne's hand, Jim asked.

"Are you expecting any trouble today Investigator Quinn?"

"Not really, but things could heat up. The suits pushing the Lily Bay development have a fancy presentation ready to go, and then it opens up for questions and comments, with lots of people, pro and con, signed up to speak."

Jim nodded and replied.

"I've been to a bunch of these town halls over the years and it's hard to guess how they're going to unfold. But I'm glad you're here."

All of the seats were taken when Jim and Doug entered, and they joined a number of other people standing along the back wall. There was a subdued tension in the room that did not bode well for the meeting, and a few anti-Lily Bay signs were scattered through the audience. Doug watched as Anne walked down the right-hand aisle and leaned casually up against the wall about halfway down toward the stage. Soon other latecomers joined her along the wall as the auditorium filled to overflowing.

A short rotund man in a tight-fitting suit approached the lectern and nervously tapped on the microphone.

"My name is Lloyd Robinson, and I've been asked by the Moosehead Lake Region Chamber of Commerce to moderate today's town hall meeting regarding the proposed development up on the east side of the lake at Lily Bay. We will start with an informative Power Point presentation of the present plans, and then people can ask questions and offer comments."

A youngish balding man in chinos, tassel loafers, and a lavender polo shirt stood up from his seat in the front row, stepped up on the stage, and approached the lectern with a smile for the crowd. Doug almost broke out laughing – what was this guy thinking? He wasn't wearing a suit, but his 'cocktails around the pool' outfit was not going to ingratiate him with the audience. An audible ripple of snickers and hisses rolled across the room as the speaker introduced himself and started the sales pitch.

As the plans for a vacation community of over 400 homes clustered at Lily Bay, one of the most beautiful and still untouched places in the region, were described in glowing terms, Doug's attention turned to Anne, leaning against the side wall of the auditorium. She looked tired, he thought, worn out. He wasn't surprised. She had been through two long winters in central Maine since moving here from Michigan, and her job as an investigator for the Piscataquis County Sheriff's Office could be a grind. It was a big county with lots of problems, and Hudson, the new sheriff, had been leaning on her hard. Anne was wearing her standard work outfit – boots, baggy Carhartt pants with a deep side pocket for her telescoping baton, and a loose flannel shirt, probably from Renys Department store down in Dexter, that covered her sidearm and badge. She could almost fade into the crowd, but her height – she was almost six feet, and her fluid grace and physicality – she had played point guard college ball in the Big Ten, drew attention, along with her natural good looks. Her blond hair was long now, he noticed, and unkempt, and her pants had mud splattered on them. She had a large bandage on the back of her left hand, and a fresh scratch on her forehead.

Doug noticed Anne shift her position on the wall and glance toward the back of the auditorium, where a man had stood up from his aisle seat and was walking down toward the stage. The man suddenly picked up his pace and started yelling about being ready to kill any "mother-fuckin tree huggers from away" that tried to block the project. He was clearly trying to reach the environmentalist opponents to the Lily Bay development who were sitting in the front row waiting for their turn to speak. Anne didn't move to block the man rushing the stage, but as he passed she stuck her foot out and tripped him. Sprawled in the aisle, with laughter erupting around him, the man was now enraged, and standing up, he turned back toward Anne, calling her a bitch and raising his open hand as if to slap her.

Anne had moved into the center of the aisle and held her now extended 21" steel baton down next to her right leg where it couldn't be seen by most of the audience. The man could see her slapping her leg with it, however. With her left hand Anne pulled back her flannel shirt far enough that he could see her badge and sidearm, but what froze him in place was the flash of silver at her belt. A deranged killer had severed part of the little finger on Anne's left hand several years back, and she had replaced it with a silver digit in emulation of Holly Hunter in the movie "The Piano." Anne's silver pinkie was pretty widely known across the county, as was her skill with a baton. She nodded her head slightly and smiled at the man, acknowledging that he had recognized her. Offering him a way out, she spoke in a calm voice that carried across the auditorium.

"Sorry for the trip. I apologize. If you would please take your seat you can offer your comments later in the program."

Lowering his arm, the man shrugged, feigning nonchalance, and walked back up the aisle and out the door of the auditorium. Anne surreptitiously slipped her baton back in its pocket and leaned back up against the wall as the presentation started back up.

Jim turned to Doug and asked.

"What just happened there? Why did he back down like that with people laughing at him?"

Keeping his eye on Anne, Doug replied.

"Well, she showed her badge and sidearm, so he realized she was law enforcement, and that any aggression on his part would likely result in some jail time. She also gave him a good look at her baton, and he must have had some prior experience with the damage they can do. But probably the most important message she sent was the waggle of her silver pinkie. He obviously realized who she was when he saw it, and what she was capable of. He didn't want to be on the receiving end of things if, as the Brits would describe it, she decided to 'put the stick about.'"

2.
ANNE
SATURDAY

Anne should have been relaxed and pleased on her drive back down to Dover-Foxcroft from Greenville later that afternoon. Except for the doofus who had tried to rush the stage, she thought that the town hall had gone better than expected. There had been some posturing and gasbagging, but mostly people had expressed thoughtful and heartfelt concerns about how the proposed development would impact Greenville and the surrounding communities. There were clearly strong feelings on both sides, and occasional outbursts of anger had occurred, but nothing approaching physical confrontation.

Her hands were trembling on the steering wheel, however, and she felt a slight wave of anxiety wash over her. She knew she had been close to losing it in the auditorium. The urge to bring the baton down on the man's upraised arm had been almost overpowering. Anne was pretty sure that only the full auditorium of onlookers had kept her from lashing out. If they had squared off in the parking lot it could well have ended differently. And it wasn't the first time in recent weeks she had come close to using force when it wasn't called for. Hudson, the new sheriff, was wearing her down with his constant belittling, verbal abuse, and shitty assignments, and with the exception of Jim Torben she was getting little support from her co-workers in the sheriff's office.

Anne was also embarrassed by how she had handled her encounter with Doug Bateman. They had worked really well together as an investigative team on the serial killer case a few years back. Their relationship had grown into what she thought was a close friendship and looked to be moving toward something more. But he had kept his distance once the case was resolved and their work lives diverged. Doug's estranged wife Beth had reappeared at about the same time and Anne had heard that they were trying again to make their marriage work. Anne had no lack of prospects for male companionship, and her friend June Torben was always trying to fix her up with local men – mostly those recently divorced or one of her distant cousins, but June also suggested on frequent occasions, to Anne's strong denials, that she was still carrying a torch of sorts for Doug Bateman.

Anne's cell phone vibrated in her shirt pocket and she pulled over just outside of Guilford to answer it. It was the sheriff's office dispatcher, directing her to the Mayo Regional Hospital in Dover-Foxcroft. Carol Merner, the hospital's sexual assault forensic examiner, had just called on behalf of an apparent rape victim who wanted to report the assault to authorities.

Carol was taking a cigarette break by the front door and gave Anne a brief rundown as they walked back to the patient's room. Except for a low background hum, the hospital corridor was silent, and Anne could hear the squeak of Carol's shoes on the brightly polished floor.

"Her name is Gayle Robertson. She came in this morning at about 9 o'clock, reported the rape, and asked for help. The assault took place last night at her home, several miles north of Dexter, where she lives alone. It's just north of the county line, so she lives in Piscataquis County, not Penobscot. She's relatively composed and readily consented to a full sexual assault forensic exam, which we finished up a few hours ago. We should have a copy of the patient assault information and inventory forms detailing our findings, along with the completed sex crimes kit, for you by later today."

Looking down at a printout, Carol continued.

"I think we were able to recover solid DNA evidence of her assailant from several sources. UV light examination fluoresced a number of blue-white smears of dried secretions, likely semen, from her inner thighs, and pubic combing provided a number of hairs that don't appear to be from her. So if the assailant is in any DNA databases we should be able to get a match. We also took urine and blood samples because she indicated that she had been drugged. In terms of physical injuries, there is some bruising on her neck indicating strangulation, so she'll be kept overnight for observation, just to make sure that no resultant breathing problems develop. We also observed distinct ligature marks on both wrists, which is consistent with her description of being tied up during the attack."

As they reached the door to the victim's room Carol handed the printout she had been consulting to Anne, along with a photograph. She then paused and shook her head slowly, the fluorescent ceiling lights reflecting off her smudged glasses.

"The neck bruising and ligature marks are fairly common in rape cases, but her other injury is not. As you can see in the photograph, she was branded. The number 9, measuring about 2" in height, was burned into the fleshy part of her right hip, just below the belt line."

Anne looked at the photo in surprise as Carol continued.

"I gotta tell you Anne, this is one of the strangest stories I have ever heard. I know she was drugged, and some of what she says might be hallucinatory memories, but she is very coherent and very clear in her description of what happened. I believe her. I know you will be going over much of the same ground we covered, but if you have any questions come find me after you talk to her."

Thanking Carol, Anne entered the room. Gayle Robertson was sitting up in bed reading a magazine, and smiled hesitantly as Anne introduced herself. Gayle was quite attractive in spite of her disheveled appearance, with short black hair, high cheekbones, and piercing gray eyes. And understandably, she was clearly scared.

"I can't believe they're insisting on keeping me here overnight. I feel fine now, and I hate hospitals. Can't I get out of here?"

Anne pulled a chair over close to the bed and put her hand on Gayle's, which she could feel was trembling.

"I know this is scary Gayle, but you did the right thing – coming straight here and asking Carol to contact the police. You're safe now, and we'll catch this creep."

"Oh, I wouldn't have come at all, but he told me to. He said he would be watching me and wanted me to get the rape kit exam and to contact the police."

Anne didn't try to hide her surprise, but instead of following up on Gayle's statement, she decided it would be better to start at the beginning and let Gayle tell her story in her own words. Reaching into her bag, Anne held up her small tape recorder.

"Gayle, if it's OK with you, I'd like to record our conversation."

Gayle nodded, and Anne asked her to just start at the beginning and tell her what happened.

"Well, I was woken out of a deep sleep by someone calling my name and shining a bright light into my eyes – a flashlight, I guess. I glanced at the clock by my bed and it was 3:33 AM, which stuck in my head for a while. I mean there's a strange man in my bedroom in the middle of the night. He knows my name and is shining a light in my eyes and here I am thinking 333 over and over. But then he held this big knife in front of the flashlight beam where I could see it, and that got my attention. I mean this knife was huge. I've never seen anything like it. It wasn't a machete or anything, but it had a big long blade and was polished. And it had blood on it. I asked about the blood and he said that there was a cat on the front porch and it was making noise, so he cut it in half and threw it into the bushes. It must have been the neighbor's cat Butch – he comes over sometimes to mooch food."

Hoping to slow down the rapid narrative, Anne asked in a soothing voice.

"Did you see at all what he looked like?"

"No, no chance. Right after he showed me the knife he threw me a blindfold, like the ones you use to sleep on a plane, and told me to put it on. Then he taped it to my head with wrapping tape or something – really tight – I couldn't see any light at all."

"Then what happened?"

"Then he told me to put my hands above my head and he tied them tight together at the wrists with some sort of slip tie – I could hear it clicking tighter. And then he fastened my arms to the bedframe somehow above my head. Once I was tied down I could hear him turn on the bedside light, and he didn't say anything for quite a while. A few minutes at least. I don't wear any pajamas or anything to bed, so I guess he was looking at my body, maybe taking pictures. I heard some clicking, like what an iPhone makes when you take a picture"

Gayle abruptly stopped talking and gazed blankly over Anne's shoulder at the far wall.

"Gayle, would you like to take a break?"

"No, I'm OK, I was just trying to remember what he said. It was so weird." Taking a deep breath, Gayle continued.

"I felt him sit down beside me on the bed, and he pulled the sheet up, tucking it in around my neck. Then he told me that he knew I was a good girl – that I went to church on Sundays and to choir practices on Wednesday nights. He also said he could tell that I was a valued employee at Renys Department Store, and was impressed by how often I worked out at Millside Fitness in Dexter. So he must have been following me around."

"Gayle, had you noticed anyone hanging around or watching you recently? Anything like that?"

"No, nothing. Then he told me – this is where it really got creepy – he told me he thought we made a great couple, that I would be a good wife, and that we could have a baby together, and we would be happy. I could tell he was dead serious and I pretty much shut down then. I was terrified. He said he had just a few questions before he took me as his wife and then asked if I used drugs or had any sexually transmitted diseases or other illnesses, and if I could have children."

Anne couldn't hide her mounting apprehension, and seeing her expression, Gayle smiled and nodded.

"I know. Fucking crazy, right? Right now I am just glad to be alive. I guess I passed his quiz – don't know what would have happened if I hadn't, and he rambled on for a while about how he really wanted kids and what a great mom I would be, and how much he loved me. Then he slipped a ring on my left ring finger and said we were married."

Anne interrupted Gayle's narrative at this point.

"Do you still have the ring?"

"No, he must have removed it when I was drugged."

"What happened then?"

"Well, then he put a pill in my mouth and gave me some water. He said it was K, whatever that is, and that it would relax me."

Anne nodded.

"K is Ketamine, Gayle. It's an anesthetic but also used recreationally, and is a common date-rape drug. It can produce agitation and hallucinations, and at high doses can create a detached, dreamlike state, making it difficult to move. Users frequently describe a trance-like out of body experience, but memory loss is also common."

"I don't remember much after that, thank goodness. He told me he was going to 'put the baby.' I could feel him pulling the sheet down and climbing on top of me. I felt really agitated, and that's when he choked me. I have a vague memory of him raping me, and even asking me, I think, if he was a good lover, and did I enjoy it? He also said that if I aborted our baby he would know and would kill me."

Gayle paused, and Anne asked.

"Do you remember him branding you?"

"I guess so. I remember him climbing off and walking out of the bedroom, and then a pressure on my right hip, and some pain, but not a lot. It wasn't until later that it really started to hurt. They have it covered now by a bandage. What's it look like?"

Anne showed her the photograph.

"A '9' – what's that supposed to mean?" Gayle asked.

Anne responded.

"I really have no idea, but we'll query our databases to see if anything similar has been reported. Do you remember much of what happened after the branding?"

"I think I was unconscious for a while. When I woke up I could hear him humming a tune. When he saw I was awake he cut the ties around my wrists and told me how much he loved me and how happy we were going to be. He told me to go to the hospital and to be sure to report it to the police – that was OK with him. Then he said he was leaving, and not to take the blindfold off until I thought a half hour had passed. He would be in touch, he said, and that he would be watching over me."

"Is there anything else you can remember?" Anne asked, "His voice, his car driving away, anything he said, anything that might help us catch him?

Gayle frowned.

"Not really. His hand felt funny when he put the pill in my mouth – I think he was wearing rubber gloves or something, and his voice was just regular – not a strong Maine accent, or any accent really. I think he shuffled his feet a bit or dragged one foot maybe. I'm just glad he didn't kill me."

Anne nodded, and asked Gayle if she had any idea why her assailant encouraged her to contact the police.

"I don't really know – it sounded like he was just trying to impress me that he was important somehow – that the police would want to know about him."

Gayle gazed over Anne's shoulder again, pensive, and continued.

"I can't go back living in that house, ever. Or back working at Renys. I'm going home to my mom and dad in Old Orchard Beach and start over. I just hope I'm not pregnant."

Anne asked if she had been counseled about her options for terminating the pregnancy if it came to that, and was surprised by Gayle's answer.

"Oh, I would never consider abortion – that would be against my faith. It would be murder."

Not knowing how to respond, Anne replied.

"Here's my card Gayle. I will probably need to talk to you again. And if you think of anything, anything at all, in the meantime, call me. We'll have someone go back to the house with you tomorrow while you collect what you need, and to see if we can find any additional evidence."

Anne gave her a brief smile and went to find Carol to see if she remembered any additional details of what Gayle had told her before heading across town to the sheriff's office.

Sheriff Hudson was looking through the few papers scattered on Anne's desk when she walked into her office.

"Can I help you find something?" she asked.

As he straightened up, Anne couldn't help thinking, for the thousandth time, what an unpleasant looking man Hudson was. Grossly overweight, his belly strained against his uniform shirt, obscuring his belt. He didn't appear to bathe very frequently and his receding hairline was slicked back with some sort of perfumed pomade. Bad teeth, close set brown eyes, and abundant ear hair rounded out an altogether unpleasant physical appearance.

Ignoring Anne's question, Hudson let his gaze slowly move up her body before asking in a high pitched, abrasive voice.

"I hear you were involved in an unpleasant altercation up at the town hall meeting in Greenville. I want a report on my desk by the end of the day explaining your actions."

Anne paused before responding, waiting for the sheriff to move out from behind her desk. She had gotten into the habit of locking her desk drawers and leaving nothing of importance out on the desktop for Hudson to see.

"No report is necessary sheriff," Anne replied. "Nothing really happened – a guy accidentally tripped and fell down, and I provided some assistance. Lots of people witnessed it."

"What took you so long coming back? I have another assignment for you – a break-in at the Lumbermen's Museum up in Patten.

Apparently some high-value items were taken."

Hudson had been going out of his way to find minor crimes, preferably at the far ends of the county, for Anne to investigate. She held up the reports Carol Merner had given her and responded.

"I was over at the hospital interviewing a rape victim. I should follow right up on it, don't you think?"

The sheriff smiled at this and nodded. He considered Anne the point person in the office for any crimes involving women, from shoplifting to domestic abuse and rape.

"I will approve that Quinn. Carry on, and keep me informed. Make sure you find out what she was wearing – maybe she was asking for it. Let's have a quick resolution – don't dawdle on this one. And head up to Patten first thing on Monday to sort out the reported break-in." Leering now, he couldn't resist adding "And there's no need for you to dress like a man. You should try wearing tight sweaters and skirts for a change."

3.
EMMA
SATURDAY / SUNDAY

Emma Lange sat on her bed in the room she was renting above the Black Frog, a waterfront restaurant located on the south shore of Moosehead Lake in the town of Greenville. It was a pretty depressing room, with a single bed, a small closet, a dresser, a threadbare carpet, and a well-worn table and chair. In the week that she had been in the room Emma had caught more than a dozen mice in the traps she set every night before going to bed, and had begun keeping a scorecard. One of the first things she had done when she moved in was to position the table and chair in front of the room's single window, which had a spectacular and unobstructed view north up the lake and also looked down on Thoreau Park and the restaurant's floating dock seating area. The view more than made up for the peeling wallpaper and abundant mouse turds.

After working as a reporter for several years at a small paper down on the coast Emma had decided to go freelance for a while, and to finally pursue her interest in the Moosehead Lake region. Her family had history here, after all, and she had long been interested in Henry David Thoreau, whose mid-19th-century journeys into the vast northern forests of Maine had started here in Greenville. Her plan was to follow Thoreau's path and to recount her adventures along the way in a blog, which could then be turned into a magazine article she wanted to pitch to *Down East* magazine.

Her idea of course was not exactly new. There had been many efforts over the past century to retrace Thoreau's routes, and sitting on the table next to her computer was a well-thumbed copy of J.

Parker Huber's classic *The Wildest Country: Exploring Thoreau's Maine.* The book was full of maps that showed the routes Thoreau followed and where he most likely camped each night. Emma's retracing of Thoreau's journey was going to be different from all the earlier travelogues, however – she was going to use it as a vehicle for considering the ongoing debate over the development project on Lily Bay. Her idea was to interweave and juxtapose Thoreau's accounts of the pristine beauty of Moosehead Lake and it's abundant plant and animal communities with detailed descriptions of what was planned in the proposed development – how the five hundred or so new high-end vacation homes would be constructed, where the marinas and golf courses would be sited, and the likely impact on Greenville and surrounding communities.

Emma had already done a lot of reading and research on the specifics of the Lily Bay project, and that afternoon's town hall meeting had yielded a wealth of additional information as well as a good cross-section of varying opinions on its positive and negative aspects. It had also provided her with an eccentric character that would add a dash of local color to her narrative. Long-winded and pompous, Richard Potter had held forth for more than a half hour at the town hall meeting, recounting his family's long history in the Moosehead Lake region, their various accomplishments and businesses, their considerable land holdings, and the prominent role he believed was his due in shaping the future of the community.

The man was a crushing bore, and clearly was not particularly popular with the audience. Potter was a small man with a short, neatly trimmed beard, and rather than standing behind the lectern, which would have mostly hidden him from view, he stood next to it as he pontificated. He wore an expensive looking three-piece suit, complete with a bright white button-down shirt, bow tie, and a pocket watch and fob. The fob chain hung across his vest and little potbelly, and a number of ornaments were suspended from it.

Midway through his speech Potter reached for the ornamented fob chain and Emma thought he was going to check his pocket watch, realize he had spoken for far too long, and bring his rambling self-indulgent narrative to a close. A chorus of groans from the audience, however, indicated something quite different. Potter proceeded to work his way from ornament to ornament along the fob chain – something he had clearly done numerous previous times in similar settings, and discussed what the ornaments signified in his family's long dynasty: a small gold fir tree, for example, represented their early and continued lumbering enterprise – their "stewardship" of the forests; a gavel marked his various ancestors who had served in elected office over the years; and a plane reflected his family's role in developing the regional airport. There were about a dozen or so ornaments on the fob chain, but fortunately Potter skipped over many of them. It was still a painful performance to sit through, and a murmur of relief and suppressed laughter rippled through the auditorium as he concluded his speech.

In spite of her negative reaction to his performance Emma had buttonholed Potter after the town hall meeting and asked if he might be available for a longer interview – that she was very interested in hearing more of his fascinating insights regarding the Lily Bay development plans and the future of the Moosehead Lake region. Potter immediately agreed, and looking up at her with a smarmy smile, suggested a dinner interview at the Black Frog.

The pier was filling up with Saturday evening diners, but Emma managed to get a table right by the water, and while waiting for Potter to show up she fed pieces of breadstick to the family of Mallard ducks that were a fixture at the restaurant. When he arrived a few minutes later Potter was wearing the same suit, and as he approached the table, Emma noticed his shoes, which appeared to have elevator heels. "Figures," she thought – a small insecure man trying to look larger, more imposing, more important, with his obviously dyed dark beard and hair, expensive suit, and the glittering array of ornaments dangling from his watch fob. She was struck by the glaring disparity between his self-image and how other people saw him. He was a little rooster of a man, posturing and preening, and as he settled into his chair Emma thought he was one of the few people she had ever met who could strut sitting down.

It wasn't long before Potter had laid the watch fob out on the table in front of her and worked his way along the entire chain of ornaments, discussing each in painful detail. Along with the fir tree, gavel, and small plane, there was an island, which Emma learned was Sugar Island, where the Potter's large summer compound was located, a disc of some sort from Potter's grandfather's service during WWII, a ship representing the family's early shipping interests on Moosehead Lake, a fish for their fish hatchery business, a maple leaf for their maple sugar company northwest of Moosehead, a moose for their hunting camps – all in all, a stunning series of boring stories.

But once Potter, or the Rooster, as Emma now thought of him, had finished with the watch fob ornaments, and his third scotch, he ran out of steam and Emma was able to start asking questions. Surprisingly, Potter turned out to know a great deal about all the ins and outs of the local political landscape, and the numerous competing interests centered on the Lily Bay development project. He was more than happy to show off and share his knowledge with Emma. She recorded it all on her phone, and by the end of the evening they had become friends of a sort. Potter suggested they might go up to Emma's room for a nightcap, and when she demurred, he gave her his card and invited her to come up to the Potter compound on Sugar Island whenever she wished – he would be there the rest of the week. Emma quickly mentioned that she would be kayaking by Sugar Island the next day and would love to stop in and take some pictures of the historic Potter compound for her blog. Potter readily agreed, and assured Emma that she couldn't miss their camp – there weren't many on the island, which was mostly public land, and theirs was the only dock along the southwest shore of the island.

The kitchen smells and noise of the Black Frog staff hustling to keep up with the dinner crowd was filtering up through the floor when Emma got back to her room, eager to write down what she had learned from Potter. She had just started taking notes on her laptop when the phone rang. It was a woman she had met a few nights earlier at the Stress Free Moose Pub down the street. Her newfound friend worked as a nurse at the Mayo Regional Hospital down in Dover-Foxcroft, and Emma had offered to treat her to dinner for any good leads on stories. Along with the Thoreau blog, Emma was always looking for other local interest stories she could sell to the contacts she had at various papers and other media outlets she knew around the state. The offer had paid off far faster than she had expected. The nurse's account of a recent rape victim's story sounded creepy enough to have real potential. Following up on the rape story would have to wait, however – Emma was setting out on a two-day solo paddle up the length of Moosehead Lake the following day, retracing the route taken by Thoreau in late July of 1857.

Emma was up early the next morning. After a breakfast of banana nut bread French toast at Auntie M's restaurant, she crossed the street and met Randy from the Kamp Kamp Indian Store, located right next to the Black Frog, who had agreed to help launch her. While Thoreau, his friend Ed Hoar, and Joe Polis, a Penobscot guide, had left Greenville in a small birch bark canoe heavily loaded with supplies, Emma would be following their route in her single person kayak, a Current Designs Slipstream model – well designed for a person her size. She had owned it for years and had thousands of hours of paddling under her belt. It didn't have much room for camping supplies, but that wouldn't be a problem. Thoreau had camped the first night at Hardscrabble Point at the north end of the Mt. Kineo peninsula, but Emma had booked a lakeside cabin at the Birches Resort, a short two-mile paddle west of Mt. Kineo on the mainland. She could reach the Birches in plenty of time for dinner and a relaxing evening watching the light fade from the lake, and the contrast between her accommodations and Hardscrabble Point would work well in her blog.

Emma was elated to get under way, and thought of Thoreau's journal entry describing his departure from Greenville in the summer of 1857: "It was inspiring to hear the regular dip of the paddles, as if they were our fins or flippers, and to realize that we were at length fairly embarked." Emma too became entranced by the rhythmic sound of her paddle as she sliced through the calm water, enveloped by the unfolding pristine beauty around her. A low morning mist still lingered on the water, and the mournful call of a loon echoed off a series of small islands close to the eastern shore of the lake.

The mist had mostly burned away by the time Emma paddled past the northernmost of the smaller islands, and she paused to take what would be the most memorable of her photos from the trip. Backlit by the gauzy rays of the rising sun filtering through the treetops of one of the islands, an elderly woman wrapped in a bright multicolored robe was sitting in an Adirondack chair set right at the water's edge. Her small cabin was just visible behind her, nestled in the shadows of the island's hemlocks and pines. She was holding a steaming cup of coffee that rested on the arm of the chair, and seated at her feet, gazing at Emma across the thirty yards of water that separated them, was a large Maine Coon cat. As Emma resumed paddling, the woman smiled and offered a casual wave, concluding their silent encounter.

When she had passed the last of the islands, Emma continued paddling almost due north, charting a course to Mt. Kineo and the Birches Resort that would take her up the middle of the lake, between Sugar Island and Deer Island. This was not the route that Thoreau's heavily loaded canoe had followed. They had turned west here and sought the wind shadow calm of the western lakeshore, which they then followed all the way up to Mt. Kineo. Emma fully appreciated the wisdom of Thoreau's Indian guide in seeking the shelter and safety of the western shore. She knew first-hand the deceptive nature of Maine's inland lakes. They were often calm in the morning, but the fickle winds of the far north could build out of nowhere, and while a lake might appear tranquil and inviting to someone standing on the shore, small whitecaps just visible farther out toward the middle of even a small lake could signal the presence of two foot rolling waves, enough to pose a serious threat to canoes, kayaks, and other small craft. This threat was compounded on Moosehead Lake for several other reasons. Not only was Moosehead larger than lakes farther south in Maine and experienced larger wave action, it was also sparsely inhabited, particularly north of Deer and Sugar Island, and watercraft in distress had much lower chances of being observed from shore. But perhaps most importantly, Moosehead Lake was colder than lakes farther south. Even the shallow waters along the lakeshore were cold enough to make your ankles ache from the cold in under a minute, and those foolhardy enough to risk full emersion invariably generated the same gasping cry, followed by a rapid rush back to dry land. Capsizing a small craft in the frigid waters of Moosehead Lake was far more than an inconvenience - it was a life-threatening event.

Emma had checked the weather forecast the night before, and it had called for light winds, less than 5 mph, up until about 3 o'clock that afternoon, when they would freshen considerably to more than 12 mph. She was confident that she would be safely at the Birches by the time the winds picked up, and had no concerns. As Emma would learn later in the day, however, the weather forecast had changed dramatically overnight.

Emma was tiring by the time she had passed Burnt Jacket Point and Sugar Island finally came into view. Potter's gossip and his family's history had kept her awake off and on throughout the night, and she was relieved to see Potter waving to her from the end of his dock. He insisted on offering her lunch on the screened porch of the main house, and her stop at Sugar Island took longer than she had planned. It was well after 2 when Emma headed north again toward Mt. Kineo and the Birches.

The wind had strengthened out of the northwest by the time she cleared the north end of Sugar Island, and she decided to continue paddling directly into the wind rather than turning west, which would have put the wind and the waves dangerously abeam. Stopping briefly to attach her kayak's skirt, which formed a barrier to water swamping it, Emma nervously eyed the darkening sky over the tree line of the distant western lakeshore. She was now in the widest part of Moosehead Lake, whitecaps were building, and the temperature was dropping. The water was now a dark gray. The spray breaking over the bow of her kayak as she plowed through the waves was cold on Emma's face, and her hands were growing numb. She couldn't help but think of the almost weekly reports of people falling out of canoes or boats during spring and early summer outings on Maine's inland lakes and succumbing to the water's icy grip.

Over the next hour Emma fought through the white-capped waves and a beating cold rain, not sure if she was making any progress against the storm. Suddenly she saw trees and a rocky shore directly ahead. She had reached Sand Bar Point and the safety of Lamb's Cove. Emma headed toward a small island in the middle of the cove, beached her kayak, and stumbled up to several tents at a campsite on the island. She was well short of Mt. Kineo and the Birches resort, but the beef stew dinner the campers shared with her was the best meal she had eaten in a long time, and as Emma snuggled into a spare sleeping bag she was grateful for her narrow escape from the icy waters of Moosehead Lake. The next morning broke clear and the lake was dead calm, with no evidence of the recent storm. Emma reached the Birches by lunchtime and after lunch and a long hot shower, she slept most of the afternoon away.

After going over her route for the next day's paddle up to the north end of the lake and the Northeast Carry landing with one of the resort's guides, Emma was relaxing in the Lodge's lounge area when the local news out of the Bangor station came on the TV. She was stunned to learn that two people had gone missing in the storm on Moosehead Lake the night before and their boat had been found washed up on shore. The search was ongoing, but they were feared dead. Tomorrow, she decided, she was definitely going to stick close to shore.

Emma had left the lounge and had been seated at a window table in the restaurant when the last story of the local news came on, so she did not hear the late-breaking report of an apparent murder victim being just discovered on Sugar Island. Two people fishing along the southwest shoreline had discovered the body of a prominent local figure – Richard Adolph Potter, at his camp late that afternoon.

4.
COWBOY
SUNDAY

From where he was parked Jimmy Bob Lentz had a clear view of the main entrance of the Charleston Pentecostal Church in the small town of Charleston, Maine, located about an hour southeast of Moosehead Lake. His Ford pickup blended well with the hundred or so other vehicles in the lot and he was parked far enough away to not draw much attention. While waiting for Sunday services to let out, Jimmy Bob was composing a wedding announcement on his laptop computer:

> Charles And Judy Robertson of Old Orchard Beach, Maine, announce the wedding of their daughter Gayle Marie, to Jimmy Bob Lentz of Cerrillos, New Mexico. The ceremony was held last evening in a private ceremony at her home north of Dexter, Maine. The bride is a graduate of the University of Maine and is currently a member of the sales staff at Renys Department Store in Dexter, Maine. The groom is the son of the cleric Abraham Lentz, patriarch of a devoted and ever-growing Christian community in Waldo, New Mexico. Mr. Lentz provides confidential professional services to a number of Fortune 500 companies. The newlyweds are praying that they will be blessed in the coming years with the procreation of a multitude of sons and daughters, who will be welcomed into the Waldo Christian Family of Heaven and Earth.

Saving the announcement to a flash drive, Jimmy Bob shut down his laptop and settled back to wait for Becky Crawford to emerge from the church. Like Gayle Robertson, Becky met Lentz's most important criteria for potential wives – she was a devoted Christian and had expressed strong opposition to abortion on her Facebook page. He invested considerable thought and effort in identifying potential wives and could not afford to waste time on someone who would not be committed to bringing their child into the world.

The front doors of the church opened and the congregation spilled out into the parking lot. Some people stopped to converse in small groups while others headed directly to their cars. Becky emerged in the midst of a group of younger parishioners who exchanged brief goodbyes and quickly dispersed to their vehicles as they reached for their cell phones. Jimmy Bob was able to take two good photos of Becky with his long lens before she reached her pickup truck. She was rather plain, he thought, but she had wide hips and would have easy deliveries. She was definitely a good bride candidate.

He was in no hurry to follow Becky and allowed several other cars to fall in behind her before he pulled out of the parking lot. Becky drove north on the Old Stagecoach Road, through Atkinson and over the Piscataquis River, and then turned east on Highway 6 at the Sebec Corners junction, heading toward Milo. If she followed her regular Sunday routine, Lentz knew she would first stop at Elaine's Café and Bakery in Milo for lunch, and then head up to the Tradewinds Market to do her weekly shopping before driving home. He figured he could stop for a quick lunch and still get to her house before she did. He pulled in at Burgers and More - a small yellow trailer parked next to the railroad tracks in Milo. Jimmy Bob was a regular customer and by the time he had parked and walked up to the counter window, the old man running the lunch joint had dropped some fresh-cut fries in the fryer and slapped a hamburger patty on the grill.

Becky shared a small house on Willow Street in Milo with her girlfriend Heather, whom she had known since high school. Heather's Honda was in the driveway when Lentz drove by the house, but Becky hadn't arrived home yet. He continued down Willow until it dead-ended and then pulled over and parked. Becky turned the corner onto Willow about ten minutes later, and Jimmy Bob slipped on his earbuds and tuned in the microphones he had installed in Becky and Heather's house. Several weeks earlier he had watched Heather hide a house key under a rock by their front door. Using it to gain entry, he had spent several hours exploring their home while they were at work.

The microphone hidden in a wall socket in the living room picked up Becky coming in the front door with several bags of groceries, and the one in the ceiling light over the kitchen table caught the conversation between Heather and Becky as they put the food away. Mostly it was chatter that Jimmy Bob wasn't interested in.

After twenty minutes of half listening to them talking, he suddenly paid close attention as Heather mentioned that her boyfriend in Bar Harbor had finally invited her to spend a long weekend with him over on the coast, and she would be gone from Thursday to Sunday. This was a big step forward in their relationship and Heather was bubbling over with enthusiasm. Lentz could tell that Becky didn't really approve of Heather's eagerness to spend three nights with her boyfriend – they weren't even engaged. Becky had pledged to remain a virgin until she was married and had been hoping to convince Heather of the importance of chastity and a firm commitment to God's teachings on the subject. Heather tolerated the sermons from Becky but so far had resisted her invitations to come with her to either Sunday services or the Wednesday night youth gatherings.

Jimmy Bob pulled out the earbuds and started up his truck, already planning the Thursday or Friday night wedding ceremony that would unite him with Becky in matrimonial bliss. He had been following several other potential brides, but Becky had just moved to the front of the line. It was a beautiful afternoon, and Lentz was in a great mood as he made the hour-long drive back up toward Greenville. He had the country and western station out of Bangor turned up loud and was singing along. Turning east off route 6 about halfway between Greenville and the small town of Shirley, he drove a few miles before turning into a long gravel drive leading back to a ramshackle farmhouse and several outbuildings. He had rented the isolated property for the summer using an alias, mailing a cashier's check to the absentee owner down in Boston.

Driving past the farmhouse, which he never used, Jimmy Bob pulled up to a sagging barn. It was a solid structure with a large set of double doors and an adjacent smaller door. He had installed a new steel hasp and padlock on the smaller door, which he now unlocked. Stepping into the dark interior of the barn Lentz closed and locked the door and punched in a four-digit code on the keypad of the security system he had installed. With motion sensors and door alarms, along with a small exterior camera hidden in the eaves above the door, the system would send an alert to Jimmy Bob's phone whenever someone approached the doors or when an intrusion occurred.

Out of habit he checked to make sure the steel bar securing the double doors from the inside was still in place before crossing over to the dust-covered RV that he called home - a Mercedes Airstream Interstate Grand Tour. It was small by RV standards but perfect for one person, and during the five years he had owned it he had modified it to suit his needs. Settling into the swivel chair at his workstation, Jimmy Bob plugged his camera into his computer and downloaded the two new photos of Becky into his Becky Crawford folder. With a rising sense of purpose he renamed the folder "10" and moved it over into another larger folder entitled "Marriages," where it joined nine other similar folders. Deleting the photos from his camera, Lentz moved the wedding announcement he had composed earlier in the church parking lot over into the folder for bride #9. There were many more weddings, and brides, than the ten Jimmy Bob had filed on his computer, but he had decided to begin a new numbering sequence a while back when he had switched over to a digital format for his record keeping, and also had begun branding his wives.

The #9 folder for Gayle Robertson was now complete, and he was looking forward to a pleasurable evening entering all the information and photos he had compiled into the "memories scrapbook" format he had developed to celebrate all of his marriages. Jimmy Bob needed to complete the scrapbook for Gayle before his marriage to Becky, which was now only a few days away. Usually his marriages were spaced a month or more apart, but he wasn't sure how long he would be staying in Maine and wanted to make sure that he wed all of the potential brides he had already identified before moving on.

In addition to Gayle and Becky, Lentz was actively tracking two other potential brides in the local area. He had initially found them both on an Internet Right to Life blog, and they more than met his standards for selection. Both were in their twenties, had a college education, regularly attended church, lacked a steady boyfriend, and lived on their own. He had opened files on both and had followed them enough to establish where they lived and worked, as well as their daily and weekly schedules. He had also researched their personal backgrounds and family history on the web and had started building their photographic archives.

Moving from his workstation over to the kitchenette, Jimmy Bob put the water on to boil, pulled a package of pasta out of the cabinet over the stove, and reached into the fridge for the container of meat sauce he had prepared a few days earlier. He was a good cook and enjoyed trying out new recipes he found online. The eggplant stir-fry dish he had seen on the Epicurious web site the day before looked interesting, but it would have to wait for now. He had too much work to do. Pouring a generous glass of his favorite Italian Barolo – which he had been surprised to find at the Shaws Market in Dover-Foxcroft, Lentz turned on a sixties rock station and returned to his desk.

Working through dinner, Jimmy Bob finished the memories scrapbook entry for Gayle Robertson #9, along with his second glass of wine, just after seven o'clock. Closing his computer, he exited the motor home, stepped out into the stillness of early evening, and started down a path toward the small stream that flowed behind the farmhouse. His right foot dragged a bit as he walked due to the damage to nerves in his leg resulting from a beating from the Patriarch he had received years ago. He no longer remembered what had incurred his anger on that particular occasion. There had been many transgressions, and many beatings, during the time he had spent with the Waldo Christian Family of Heaven and Earth.

Dappled sunlight filtered down through the trees, a hermit thrush was holding forth from some distance away, and several red squirrels began scolding him from branches overhanging the path. All in all, things were going great, Jimmy Bob thought – his search for brides was progressing extremely well, and the next few days held the promise of another wedding and another begetting. He sat for a few minutes by the stream in his usual place on a fallen log, listening to the soothing sound of the water and visualizing his upcoming wedding. Returning to the barn, he began to pull together his wedding night essentials.

Over a number of years the Patriarch had drilled into him the habits of an ordered and reverent Christian existence. Now that he was beyond the reach of the Waldo, New Mexico, Christian Family of Heaven and Earth, he ignored most of their teachings, but some stuck with him. He always said a brief prayer before meals and before turning in each evening, for example, and every morning he still made his bed with tight hospital corners, a habit that had been reinforced during his time in military service.

The battered leather suitcase Jimmy Bob slid from under his neatly made bed was one of the few things he still had from his years living in the Waldo compound. He thought of it as a hope chest of sorts. Carefully organized and curated in an upper compartment were his memorabilia from each of his weddings – keepsakes that reminded him of his brides. There were the branding irons he had made himself to sanctify the ceremonies, pairs of panties, along with locks of hair, a tooth, a bedroom slipper, earrings, and a few pieces of ear cartilage. Prior to switching over to branding, Jimmy Bob had earmarked his brides in the manner that had been used for cattle during the era of open range.

Reaching into the case Jimmy Bob removed the bulky backpack that would hold what he would need for his upcoming wedding. Placing it on the floor he started filling it with other items from the case: a blindfold of thick black felt, a roll of duct tape, a package of large zip lock ties, several lengths of cord, a pair of latex gloves, a high intensity tactical LED flashlight, a package of ketamine tablets, a small branding iron with the numeral "10," and a wedding ring, still in its red velvet box. Each of these items was fitted into the backpack in a specific order and occupied a particular place. Once the matrimonial ceremony was under way he would be able to access each without taking his eyes off his bride to be.

The final item to go into the backpack, right next to the flashlight, was his custom made Dundee Style Bowie Knife. Made by Cote Custom knives in Elliott Lake Ontario, it had a black Indian ebony handle and a front brass guard shaped like a crocodile tooth. Most importantly for his purposes was the knife's broad, brightly polished 11-inch steel blade. Jimmy Bob preferred a standard Marine issue Ka Bar fighting knife for any serious engagements, but the large polished blade of the Bowie Knife was perfect for gaining and keeping the attention of his fiancés. When he held it in front of the flashlight where they could see it, they invariably quieted right down into respectful silence and followed his instructions.

Zipping up the backpack, Lentz slid it and the suitcase back under the bed, poured himself another glass of wine, and settled in on the couch for a few hours of television. He decided to watch the last two episodes of Mindhunter. The final episode, where the FBI profiler suddenly realized how close to death he was at the hands of a serial killer, was, Lentz thought, a good conclusion. It reaffirmed his belief that law enforcement officers, even the elite behavioral profilers of the FBI, were no match for superior intellects like himself.

Turning off the TV, Jimmy Bob realized he was ready to call it a day, but then remembered he had wanted to see if he could find any information on the woman he had noticed at the Town Hall meeting in Greenville the previous day. He often frequented community meetings, as they were a great way to survey the local population of potential brides. The woman had attracted his attention not because she appeared to fit his potential bride profile but because she clearly was someone that he would be well advised to avoid at all costs.

She was older than his usual brides, and he doubted very much that she was the religious type. She was also with local law enforcement, based on the badge and gun she displayed on her belt as she pulled her coat back. Jimmy Bob was drawn to her casual threat of bodily harm and the clear message the snick of her extended baton made to the man rising to his feet to attack her. She was no Gayle or Becky, or any of the other meek vessels he had married. It would be dangerous, reckless even. He would have to be very careful with her, but he knew, as he watched her leaning against the wall of the auditorium, that she would bear him a healthy baby boy.

He googled the Greenville Police Department first, but they didn't have any female officers. He hit pay dirt with his next search – the Piscataquis County Sheriff's Department. Anne Quinn, he learned, was an investigator, but the web site didn't have much more information on her. A general Internet search on her name, however, generated a large number of local newspaper accounts of her central role in tracking down a serial killer a while back. Jimmy Bob became even more interested as he realized that she was even more dangerous than he had initially thought. Searching further, he found even older articles that documented her athletic success in college as a Big Ten basketball player, some of which provided background on her early years growing up in Michigan.

Closing out his Internet search, Jimmy Bob opened his folder on prospective brides and created a new file – Anne Quinn. Tomorrow he would drive down to Dover-Foxcroft, the county seat, and stake out the sheriff's department to begin his research on Investigator Quinn. It shouldn't be too difficult to find out where she lived and to start documenting her patterns of movement. He was pretty much free for the next four days, until his wedding with Becky. He could follow his other two prospective brides on and off through the week and still make time to build his file on Quinn. Right now she was at the bottom of his list, since he had so little information, but she could easily move up the rankings. Maybe it was time for him to take on more of a challenge. He thought he was ready.

5.
DOUGLAS
MONDAY

Doug Erving and his wife Nancy were up from Bangor for a three-day weekend of fishing on Moosehead Lake. They had trailered their 16-foot Lund outboard behind his pickup and launched from the boat ramp at Lily Bay State Park, where they had a prime walk-in tent site on Dunn Point. Their plan was to use the trolling motor to work their way slowly along the Moosehead shoreline, casting toward shore for smallmouth bass. On Saturday and early Sunday they had good luck in the many shallow water inlets of Lily Bay, east from the state park. But late in the day Sunday Nancy and Doug were forced off the lake by a strong afternoon thunderstorm.

The weather had cleared by Monday morning and they shifted their attention to Sugar Island, just north of the park. In the morning they worked their way along the east side of the island before breaking for lunch back at their campsite. In the afternoon they shifted to the south and southwest shorelines of the island and had good initial success around McCuller and Dollar Island.

Continuing clockwise along the shore, they passed several summer cabins, and were almost to Ship Island when they approached a larger compound that included a large main cabin that looked to date back to the 1920s at least, as well as a number of smaller outbuildings and a large dock. Doug steered their boat in closer to see if they could attract any bass lurking under the dock. Usually it was just bluegills that rose to their bait from under docks, but occasionally a big lunker would be lured out of the shadows.

Glancing toward the main cabin, Nancy was admiring the large screened porch when she noticed, just off to the left of the cabin, what looked like a small man with his arms wrapped around a pine tree. He was naked except for a pair of darkish boots, and it looked like he had something sticking out of the back of his head.

Doug Bateman was working through paperwork at the Major Crimes Unit North offices in the Bangor Barracks of the Maine State Police when his partner Tom Richard called to him from across the room.

"Hey Doug, we have a call on line two from the Greenville PD. Sounds like they have a body for you to look at."

Doug saw the smirk on Tom's face and frowned, realizing that since his partner was once again on desk duty due to a pending internal investigation of his apparent use of excessive force in making an arrest, Doug would have to handle yet another case by himself. He picked up the phone on his desk.

"Bateman, MCU. What's up?"

"Doug, it's Chief Marcus. We got a 911 call from a couple of fishermen up off Sugar Island just before noon, reporting an apparent body tied to a tree. We sent the launch up to check it out, and it's definitely a homicide. We didn't go ashore, so the crime scene is still intact. We can keep it undisturbed until you get up here with the Evidence Response Team."

"OK, We're on it. I should be up there by 4 at the latest. I'll call when I pass through Shirley and the launch can come back to pick me up. I'm not sure how quickly the ERT can get up there, but we have another six hours of daylight so they should make it before sundown."

Ending the call, Doug looked over to his partner Tom, shook his head, and thinking that it wouldn't hurt to try, called Stan Shetler, the head of the Major Crimes Unit.

"Lieutenant Shetler, it's Doug Bateman. There's been a homicide up at Moosehead Lake, and it sounds like it's going to be a complicated case. I really need Tom Richard to help on this. Can he be released from desk duty?"

There was a long pause before Doug received the officious response he expected.

"Absolutely not, Bateman. The accusations pending against your partner are serious. You know the regulations and procedures, and I cannot bend the rules just because we are short staffed. And there is no one else available, so don't ask. The Fentanyl Task Force is still our top priority, so you are just going to have to handle it alone."

Ending the call, Doug looked up the number for the Piscataquis County Sherriff's Office. If Shetler couldn't spare anyone to help on the Sugar Island case, maybe Sheriff Hudson could be talked into assigning Anne Quinn to team up with him. After all, Doug thought, he had teamed up with her on a high profile serial killer case a while back, and they had worked well together. As he waited to be connected to the Sheriff, Doug's heart rate suddenly spiked, and he realized how much he wanted to team up with Anne again. And it wasn't just because he had great respect for her investigative skills. He had mostly been successful putting her out of his mind, but now his intense feelings for her came flooding back.

Hudson listened to his pitch without saying anything, and then bluntly rejected it.

"Sorry Bateman. No can do. Not a chance. Quinn's on thin ice as it is and needs to definitely up her game before I would consider assigning her to a homicide. Right now she has her hands full with a break-in at the Lumbering Museum up in Patton and a rape case down by Dexter. To be honest I'm not sure why she was hired in the first place, other than her nice ass. But I can understand why you want her working with you. I bet she would do anything for you to get assigned to your murder case. But it ain't gonna happen unless you can somehow link her current cases to yours. Good luck with that."

Hudson hung up before Doug could respond. He knew that any pushback he offered would only make things worse for Anne. Before heading up to Moosehead Doug asked his partner Tom Richard to contact Peter Martell, head of the State Police Evidence Response Team, to see how quickly the ERT could join him at the crime scene. Martell called Doug back within a few minutes to let him know that his team was just finishing up with an apparent suicide of a prominent politician over in Camden and could meet him in Greenville in about two hours.

Doug was met by the Greenville Police launch at the Black Frog restaurant dock, and the ERT arrived a few minutes later. The lake was calm, with a light breeze out of the west, and the temperature was in the low 70s. They reached the camp on Sugar Island in good time, and the body of Richard Potter was clearly visible from the dock. As they approached it a swarm of blowflies rose from the body with an excited thrum.

Richard Potter's body was pressed up against the tree in a standing position with his arms wrapped around it. His wrists were tied together with a length of red nylon line and appeared to be the only thing holding him upright. What had been thought to be a pair of boots when viewed from a distance was a dark reddish-blue discoloration of his legs below the knees where blood had pooled after death. There was a large gaping wound angled diagonally across the nape of his neck which had severed his spinal cord. The back of Potter's skull was split open and the head of an axe was still deeply embedded in the wound. The axe handle angled down toward the ground at about a 45-degree angle.

Martell stepped up to the body, turned on a compact video camera, and began recording his examination of the corpse.

"Pronounced lividity in lower extremities does not disappear when pressed, suggesting that death occurred more than eight hours ago. Minimal bleeding from neck and head wounds, along with livor mortis, indicates that the victim was killed in the position we found him, and that death was instantaneous. Rigor mortis appears to be disappearing from face and neck, but is still present in larger muscle groups, suggesting death occurred twenty four to thirty six hours ago."

Taking a scalpel from his crime scene kit, Martell made a small incision in the upper right abdomen of the body and inserted a thermometer into the corpse's liver.

"Liver temperature is 73 degrees, comparable to the ambient temperature of the crime scene, which suggests that death occurred more than twenty to twenty four hours ago. There are also larva 1 stage blowfly maggots in both wounds."

Turning off the camera, Martell gave Bateman and the team a quick summary.

"The chief medical examiner will of course provide a formal assessment after the autopsy regarding the cause and time of death, but it looks pretty clear that the victim was first tied to the tree and then killed, and that the initial stroke of the axe, diagonally across his neck, killed him instantly. And if the axe in his head also caused the neck wound, then obviously the blow to the head was post-mortem. Judging from lividity, rigor mortis, liver temperature, and blowfly larval stage evidence, I would estimate that death occurred more than twenty four hours ago, but less than thirty six – so he was killed sometime from early morning to mid-afternoon on Sunday. Also, the soil under his feet, and the tree where he is pressed up against it are bone dry, which suggests he was killed before the storm hit on Sunday."

Martell turned to Doug and asked.

"Do we know who the victim is?"

Doug nodded.

"It's Richard Potter. He gave a long boring speech at the town hall meeting on Saturday – arguing against any development at Lily Bay and in support of more sensitive lumbering practices. I guess you could call him a tree hugger, although he mostly talked about himself. Given the fact that he was literally hugging a tree when he was murdered and that an axe was the murder weapon of choice, the killer could be sending a blatant anti-environmental message. There's no lack of frustrated, out of work folks around here whose livelihood is tied to the lumbering industry and who might be looking for an outlet for their anger."

Martell turned to the Greenville police officer that had piloted them out to the island.

"You had a thunderstorm up here Sunday didn't you?"

"Yes sir, we certainly did - quite a storm. Several people killed, some trees and power lines down, and a heavy rain for over an hour."

Martell walked toward the main cabin, looking around at the ground.

"We'll do a full search of the area but there's no chance of any footprints surviving the storm, and not much chance of prints or DNA either. We can bag up the body and his clothes, along with the axe and cord for transport down to Augusta for the post-mortem. Maybe we'll have better luck in the cabin."

The door to the cabin was unlocked, but nothing seemed disturbed inside. A thin layer of dust covered the massive dining table and kitchen counters, suggesting that the camp was little used. But the sink contained two unwashed plates and wine glasses, along with two place settings. The refrigerator was empty except for an almost empty bottle of sauvignon blanc and several takeout containers from the Kraken Seafood Restaurant in Greenville.

Closing the refrigerator door, Doug speculated out loud to Peter Martell.

"Looks like Potter might have opened camp for a very secluded Sunday lunch of chilled lobster and white wine. My guess is that a special lady friend was invited. But it seems that postprandial, things didn't go as planned."

Peter walked over to the sink.

"Could be. I'd bet the autopsy shows a belly full of lobster and wine – that will help to pin down when he was killed. And we'll be closer to knowing who his lunch companion was once we check the plates and wine glasses for latent prints. I'll have them boxed up for the cyanoacrylate-fuming chamber down in Augusta. The dust layer in here will make it easy for us to know where else to look for prints. It should take us another hour or so to wrap things up. You can send the launch back for us if you're finished here."

Doug nodded and stepped outside. Jay Marcus, the Greenville Police Chief answered on the first ring, and agreed to wait for Doug at the Black Frog restaurant so they could discuss the case. Doug didn't see Marcus at the Black Frog's dock and headed for the restaurant's front door. Once inside there was a long corridor leading back to the restaurant. Its walls were covered with vintage photographs that showed various groups of lumbermen and timber harvesting scenes spanning the past hundred years, and Doug always paused to look at them and search the list of names in the captions for the ancestors of people he knew.

He found Jay Marcus seated at a table on the dock, away from the other customers. They both ordered Alagash White on draft, and Doug gave a detailed account of what they had found at the Sugar Island crime scene.

Looking down at the notes he had taken, Marcus outlined what he thought they needed to do next.

"It's not going to be easy tracking down any potential witnesses to the crime. We'll get the list of campers registered at the Lily Bay State Park and question them for you, and also talk to the couple that found him as well as the camp owners along the south shore to see what they may have seen over the weekend. We can also check the Blair Hill Inn and Beaver Cove webcams – they might show something. But the killer could have accessed the island anywhere by boat and then walked to Potter's place."

"Thanks Jay," Doug responded. "What can you tell me about Richard Potter? Does he have any enemies? Anyone have it in for him?"

"Well, there's a long list of people that little Rick – that's what people call him around here, has pissed off or cheated over the years. You won't see too many mourners at his funeral. People who worked for him in his lumbering business have a lot of stories to tell about unsafe working conditions, worn out equipment, and him cheating them out of the pay they earned doing hard, dangerous work in the woods. The guy who tried to rush the stage at the town hall meeting, for example, John Shea, has had a grudge against Potter for years, and after he's had too much to drink frequently threatens to kick his ass."

Marcus paused briefly and laughed to himself.

"Then there's the business partners he apparently screwed over on the planned airport expansion – I think that court case is still ongoing. And of course his divorce a while back was particularly nasty. So your list of potential suspects will be a long one."

"How about anti-environmental sentiment – was Potter a strong advocate for conservation issues?"

"I guess you could say that. But he wasn't an outspoken leader with a specific agenda. As you no doubt could tell from his town hall talk, he is mostly interested in how wonderful he is."

"How about current female companionship?" Doug asked. "It looks like he might have had a lunch date with someone on Sunday."

Marcus leaned back in his chair, momentarily gazed up the lake, and gave Doug a big smile.

"I was wondering when you were going to get around to asking about Potter's girlfriends, or lack thereof, and who the mystery woman might be. Potter hasn't kept the company of anyone local for quite a while. Nobody can stomach his nonstop self-admiration for very long. But I do have a name for you. The leading candidate for Potter's Sunday lunch companion could be watching us right now, from a room she rents above the Black Frog."

Marcus paused, enjoying Doug's sudden intense interest, and let the suspense build as he took a long sip of his beer before continuing.

"Her name is Emma Lange. She's been in town for at least a few weeks. I think she's a journalist from Down East and apparently is working on yet another article about Thoreau's travels in the Maine woods back in the 1850s."

"What's her connection to Potter?" Doug asked.

"I don't think there was one until the Saturday town hall meeting. I saw her corral Potter afterward and she seemed very interested in what he had to say. She's probably hoping to do a story on the Lily Bay development plans. He must have invited her to have dinner with him – I heard they ate here on Saturday night and that she was recording their conversation and seemed to be hanging on every word."

"Definitely interesting," Doug responded. "But it still doesn't put her on Sugar Island having lunch with Potter."

"I wasn't quite finished Doug. Sunday morning I saw Emma having breakfast at Auntie M's – looked like French toast. She had a kayaking outfit on and I watched Randy from Kamp Kamp help launch her right off the dock here. I asked him later where she was going and he said she was doing a two-day paddle - following Thoreau up to Mt. Kineo, and then on to the Northeast Carry. She also told Randy that she thought she would paddle up the east side of the lake, right past Sugar Island."

Doug motioned their waiter over to the table.

"Chief Marcus, I would like to buy you another beer."

6.
EMMA
TUESDAY / WEDNESDAY

Driving back from the north end of Moosehead Lake late on Tuesday, Emma turned on the radio just south of Kokajo and heard a brief news report about the death of Richard Potter. Half an hour later she pulled into the Greenville Police Department parking lot. She told the officer at the front desk that she had information regarding the Potter homicide and asked to see someone involved in the investigation. Jay Marcus talked to her briefly, called Doug Bateman down in Bangor, and arranged for her to return the next morning to be formally interviewed.

When she arrived Wednesday morning, Chief Marcus led Emma back to a small interview room.

"Have a seat Ms. Lange, Detective Bateman will be with you in just a few minutes."

Emma sat at a metal table that was bolted to the floor and had a large ring welded into the top for securing prisoner restraints. It was a small windowless room with a concrete floor and cinderblock walls painted an institutional green. The air was stale and the fluorescent ceiling light flickered on and off at irregular intervals, generating an irritating buzz. A small video camera mounted on the wall near the ceiling next to the door was pointed straight at her. Emma looked up at its red flashing light and realized that someone was probably watching her on a screen in another room. She thought about waving at the camera, but realized her hands were suddenly shaking. She had never been in a police station before, never been questioned by a detective, and never been in a room like this one.

She wanted out. Out into the fresh air and the sunshine. Fifteen minutes passed and Emma took her windbreaker off – she was warm and couldn't seem to steady her hands, so she clenched them on her lap under the table.

Emma jumped when the door suddenly opened and Doug Bateman walked in, taking the chair across from her.

"Sorry to keep you waiting Ms. Lange. I had a few things to check on. Thanks for calling and offering to help us in our investigation." Doug smiled and opened a folder on the table in front of him and turned on a small tape recorder, dictating the day and time, and their names.

"My name's Douglas Bateman. I'm a detective with the Major Crimes Unit of the Maine State Police and am heading up the investigation of the homicide of Richard Potter."

Emma started to relax a little. Bateman was dressed casually in a dark green rolled neck wool sweater and was handsome in a rugged way, with black hair and bright blue eyes. He had a quiet, calm way of talking that encouraged her to confide in him. She took out her phone, held it up for Doug to see, and he nodded his approval. She turned on the audio recording function and placed it on the table. Her hands had stopped shaking.

"How long have you been in Greenville, Ms. Lange?"

"A few weeks. I have a room above the Black Frog."

"What brought you to town?"

"I'm a journalist. I've worked down on the coast for several years and came up here to do a free-lance piece juxtaposing Thoreau's travels in the region with the Lily Bay development plans."

"How long have you known Richard Potter?"

"Just since Saturday. I met him after the town hall meeting."

"And you had dinner with him at the Black Frog on Saturday night?"

Emma was surprised by the question and stumbled as she responded.

"Ah.... Yes. He invited me to dinner and I accepted. He seemed to be a good source for my story."

"And what kinds of things did you talk about? Can you remember?"

"Actually, detective, I recorded the entire dinner conversation on my phone. If you want, I can download it to one of your computers before I leave today."

It was Doug's turn to be caught by surprise and Emma smiled at his reaction.

"That would be a big help to us Ms. Lange. Thank you."

Doug continued his questioning.

"What happened after your dinner Saturday night with Potter?"

"Well, as you will be able to tell from the recording, he was quite impressed with himself and after dinner he tried to invite himself up to my room. I deflected his advance and we tentatively agreed that we would get together for lunch the next day – Sunday, at his camp on Sugar Island. He left and I went up to my room to listen to the recording and work up my questions for him for the next day."

"The next day you had breakfast at Auntie M's – French toast I think. And after breakfast, Randy from Kamp Kamp helped to launch you in your kayak. Where were you headed?"

Again, Emma was surprised at what Doug already knew.

"It was a two-day paddle up to the Northeast Carry, spending the first night near Mt. Kineo. I was following Thoreau's journey of 1857, but took a slightly different route. I went up past Sugar Island rather than along the west side of the lake, so stopping at Sugar Island was not out of the way."

Doug raised his hand to stop Emma's narration.

"You had lunch with Potter on Sugar Island on Sunday?"

"Yes."

"OK. Great. We'll come back to that in a bit. What happened after that?"

"I got caught in the storm before I reached Mt. Kineo. It came up fast and it was bad - really scary. I made it to Lamb's Cove, south of Kineo on the west side of the lake, and some campers there took me in and shared their food and tent with me."

"Do you remember their names, where they were from?"

"Yes, of course – his name was Doug Price and he called his wife Gitte. They were from Madison, Wisconsin. They might still be at the campsite. It was on an island in the middle of the cove."

"OK. Go on."

"The next morning I paddled up to the Birches, just west of Mt. Kineo. I got there about noon, had lunch, and then slept most of the rest of the day. The next day - yesterday, I paddled up to the Northeast Carry, picked up my car, and drove back down to Greenville."

Emma paused, and Doug took her back to Sugar Island.

"About what time did you arrive at Potter's on Sunday?"

"I'm not exactly sure. I would guess about noon. It was easy to find. There aren't many camps on the southwest shore of the island, and Potter was watching for me from his dock."

"Then you had lunch?"

"Yes. He showed me around his camp and then we had lunch on the screened porch. A great lunch – cold lobster and white wine, and a flan for dessert."

"What did you talk about?"

"Well, like the dinner the evening before, he mostly talked about himself, and I tried to get him to talk about Lily Bay and what people thought about it."

Emma smiled coyly and continued.

"I also taped our lunch conversation and will download it for you if you like."

"Thanks, that would be very helpful," Doug replied. "And after lunch?"

"After we finished eating I helped him clear the table, we put the dishes in the sink, and then he invited me to stay for the afternoon, maybe go swimming or for a walk. He was pretty blatant about what he was really interested in but didn't push it when I told him I really had to press on."

"So you left soon after lunch? About what time was that?"

"I'm not sure – probably about one thirty, maybe two."

"And when did you reach Lamb's Cove."

"Again, I'm not exactly sure. Four maybe. It was dark because of the storm, so difficult to estimate the time. And it's easy to lose track of time in rough water."

Doug looked down at his list of questions.

"Did you see anyone else while you were at Potter's place or while you were nearby in your kayak - people either on land or in other watercraft?"

"A few boats went by while we were having lunch, and I saw someone fishing from a canoe farther up the shoreline after I left. Oh, and the vintage tour boat Katahdin went by on one of its Sugar Island cruises just as I was leaving. That's about it."

"Did Potter seem worried about anything? Did he mention anyone who might have a grudge against him, or any problems he was dealing with?"

"No, not really. You can tell from the tapes he was very relaxed and upbeat."

Doug closed the folder in front of him on the table and slowly got to his feet, as if he was trying to think of any questions he had missed.

"I guess that's all the questions I have for you right now Ms. Lange. There may be more I need to ask you, so let's get your phone number, email address, and other contact information. And let's find a computer to download the recordings you made of your conversations with Potter. They're going to be a big help. We'll also need to take your fingerprints before you leave."

After Emma had left the station Doug sat down with Chief Marcus to go over the interview. They both thought she seemed credible, and not a likely suspect. She had only known Potter for a little over twenty four hours, and the recordings of the conversations she had with him would go a long way toward confirming her explanation of what she was doing on Sugar Island shortly before he was killed. Her timeline for Sunday also seemed reasonable, given the distances she had paddled and the difficult paddling conditions in the rough water on Sunday afternoon.

Chief Marcus agreed to interview John Shea, who had rushed the stage at the town hall meeting, to see what his alibi was for Sunday afternoon. He would also try to track down the campers she had encountered in Lamb's Cove and see if they remembered when she had arrived, and to also check at the Birches to see if her story held up there. And the Moosehead Maritime Museum should be able to tell them what time the Katahdin, a 102-foot long steamship built in 1914 and still providing tours of Moosehead Lake, would have passed by the southwest shoreline of Sugar Island on Sunday. Maybe one of the crew had noticed Emma and Potter, and if she was in fact just setting off when they went by. Such a sighting would both support her timeline and if Potter was alive when she left, further take her out of the running as a suspect. It would also narrow down the window of when he was killed – after Emma had left and before the storm hit Sugar Island.

On his end, Doug would have his partner Tom Richard run a check on Emma's background – her family and work history, and anyone who could corroborate her motivations for coming to Greenville. They would also get a list of Potter's disgruntled business associates from Marcus and interview them, and check into his financial situation. And Doug was expecting to hear from Tom that afternoon regarding the results of the autopsy, and any updates on the axe and the cord used to tie Potters hands.

As Doug got up to leave he assured Marcus that he would check in with him daily so they could share information, and left the chief with a final question.

"One thing that puzzles me – why didn't Ms. Lange ask any questions at all about how Potter was killed? You would think she would want to know, particularly being a journalist."

Marcus agreed.

"That is surprising. Maybe we shouldn't be too quick to clear her as a suspect just yet."

After having her fingerprints taken Emma stepped out the front door of the police station into the bright sunshine of a beautiful Maine afternoon, took a deep breath, and started walking back to the Black Frog. The detective had seemed nice, but she didn't like his questions and his way of watching her so intently, like he could see what she was thinking and what she wasn't telling him. She decided that a reward was in order for surviving that horrible little room and the scary interview and thought that a large soft serve cone from the Dairy Bar across from the Kamp Kamp store was just the thing.

Holding a large chocolate cone, she crossed the street, dodged the logging trucks and tourist traffic, and sat on one of the benches in the small Thoreau Park that was wedged between the Kamp Kamp store and the Black Frog. She had realized last night that her planned blog about Thoreau and Lily Bay would have to wait. This Potter murder was a big story and she was perfectly positioned to cover it. Everyone at the Black Frog was talking about the murder the previous evening, and she had joined the group in the bar that was crowded around one of the officers who had been at the crime scene as he held forth in great and gruesome detail about the naked victim hugging a tree and with an axe sticking out of his head.

Emma was confident that some of the big papers – the Boston Globe was her first choice, would be interested in the story, particularly given her recordings of conversations with Potter rambling on about Lily Bay and a wide range of other topics, and her lobster and white wine lunch with him just prior to his killing. She thought the gruesome nature of the crime would be the kicker – axe murders made for good stories. Finishing her ice cream she started back to her room, already thinking about how to pitch the story to the Globe. First she would have to listen again to the recordings to see if there were any hints about motive for the crime. And she would also have to try to get the police to confirm details of the killing. A drunk in a barroom crowd bragging about what he saw didn't qualify as a "well placed police official speaking on the condition of anonymity."

Doug's partner Tom Richard called him later that afternoon with the results of the Potter autopsy.

"A few surprises, Doug. The victim was apparently first struck with a blunt object on the back of the head – compressed skull fracture – probably the back end of an axe head – about the right size and shape. The chop to the neck killed him, then the axe into the skull. Here's a surprise though. Two different axes were used, based on the wounds. A felling or cutting axe, with a shallower wedge angle on the blade, was used on the nape of his neck, but the axe left in his head is a splitting axe, with a deeper wedge angle. So the killer switched weapons during the murder, and only left one at the scene."

Doug responded.

"We'll have to go back and do a wider search at the crime scene, particularly in the water. The killer may have thrown the second axe into the lake."

Tom continued.

"It gets more interesting. The splitting axe – the one left at the scene, is not an axe you can pick up at Lowes or Home Depot – it's an older axe – vintage. I just sent you some photos of it as email attachments. But it's not going to be easy tracking it down. I talked briefly to someone at Brant and Cochran, the axe company down in Portland, and they said vintage axes have become very popular and there are a wide variety being bought and sold. Apparently more than 300 different axe manufacturers existed in Maine between 1800 and 1960. He suggested we talk to the curator up at the Lumbermen's Museum in Patten."

"I can do that," Doug replied, and called the museum as soon as he and Tom ended their call.

Once Doug got the curator on the phone, she sounded skeptical about the likelihood of providing much information of any value to the investigation.

"There are tens of thousands of old axe heads around, many of which don't have their original handles. They come in a wide variety of different styles or types, and from hundreds of different manufacturers over the past 150 years. Sometimes they have maker's marks but often they don't. If you can send me a picture I'll see what I can do. But I can't promise anything."

Doug thanked her and forwarded on the pictures Tom had just sent him.

The curator called back within a few minutes, sounding quizzical, and a little irritated.

"OK. Here's what I can tell you about the axe in the photos you sent me. It's a splitting axe, with a deep wedge angle. The bit has a simple Maine pattern shape. This particular axe was manufactured in 1943 by the Emerson & Stevens Company in Oakland Maine, likely under the Lumberman's Pride brand name. The handle is original, maple, made by Gammon Handle in Lovell, right over by the Vermont border. It is one of a few hundred ordered by the federal government for their lumbering camps. Will that help?"

Puzzled both by the detail the curator was able to provide, and the obvious edge to her description, Doug replied.

"Thanks very much. But I thought you said you probably wouldn't be able to provide much information. How could you tell so much just from the photos?"

"You really don't know, do you? Don't you people ever talk to each other? That axe is one of two that were stolen from one of our exhibits last week. An investigator from the Piscataquis County Sheriff was just up here this morning taking the report. Maybe you should talk to her – Quinn was her name. Do you have the other axe by any chance – a very nice felling axe from the same time period – in good condition, with a hickory handle? When can we get them back?"

Doug replied that they would need to keep the splitting axe, as it was evidence in a criminal case, and promised to let the curator know if they recovered the felling axe. Thanking the curator again, he also said he would be in touch with Investigator Quinn.

7.
ANNE
WEDNESDAY

Anne had spent most of Monday and Tuesday in bed nursing a cold, and still felt pretty sketchy as she drove north on I95 Wednesday morning to interview the director and curator of the Patten Lumbermen's Museum about the burglary they had reported the previous week. The gray overcast sky matched Anne's mood.

A few years back she had left the bustling college town of Ann Arbor Michigan and her promising job with the police department there to start a new life in central Maine. Now she wasn't so sure she had made the right choice.

On the positive side of things, the camp Anne had bought and refurbished on the south shore of Sebec Lake felt like home now and she looked forward to her summer evening ritual of taking a glass of Sauvignon blanc out to the end of her dock and watching the sun go down. Her large white tomcat Charles would often follow her out and perch on the arm of her chair. There was always some sort of entertainment on offer – boats pulling tubes of children, shrieking with excitement, the slow progress of loon pairs calling to each other and disappearing below the surface of the lake for minutes at a time, the raucous cry and dipping flight of the resident kingfisher as he patrolled the shoreline, cat's paws moving across the lake in the fading light.

Anne had also begun to feel more at home in the community. She had formed a close friendship with June Torben, who was married to the Chief Deputy in the sheriff's office, and she had dinner at the Torben's every week or so. People in Dover-Foxcroft, the town of

5,000 that was the county seat or "shire town" had also begun to consider her as a local rather than being "from away," and she had gotten to know many of the parents of the Lady Ponies – the girls basketball team at the local high school - Foxcroft Academy. Anne had played college ball at the University of Michigan and had started a summer program of informal practices with the team on a seldom-used court behind a local church.

Most Saturday mornings she also met up with a half dozen or so other serious cyclists from the local area for a good thirty mile ride over the rolling hills along the Piscataquis River Valley. Until a month or so ago Anne had been the strongest rider in the group, but now she was challenged to keep up with a newcomer – Colin Watson. He was a businessman of some sort over in Bangor - single, about Anne's age, and drove over on weekends to ride with the group. He was a few inches taller than Anne and had the well-toned muscles and low body fat index of a serious athlete. With an easy laugh, dark green eyes, a British accent, and red hair, he had quickly blended in with the other riders.

Anne knew that there were other, better cycling clubs that Colin could be riding with in Bangor, and it was pretty obvious to Anne, and to the other riders in the group, that he had joined them because of her. The teasing had already started regarding how long it would be before he worked up the nerve to ask her out. Anne suspected that he slacked off on the flats, riding just fast enough to make her work hard to keep up with him, but then would slow on the climbs, allowing her to pass and lead him up the hills. He claimed he wasn't a good climber but the women in the group thought he just enjoyed the view from behind as Anne stood on her pedals and powered up the inclines. Her best friend June Torben had of course learned about the potential new man in Anne's life. June had googled Colin and learned he was a well-heeled media mogul, leading her to urge Anne with increasing frequency to give him some encouragement.

Cruising along at 75 mph Anne was making good time on the interstate. Sitting up straighter, she tried to find a comfortable position, but the springs in the driver's seat of her mid-70s vintage Toyota Land Cruiser were shot and any trip over twenty miles was now uncomfortable. Her dad had left her the land cruiser in his will and she prided herself on keeping it well maintained. But it was closing in on two hundred thousand miles, and it seemed like she was replacing something on it every month. Anne knew that she would have to find another vehicle before winter arrived.

It represented one of the last physical links to her family and her youth in Manistee, Michigan, and she hated to relegate it to summer weekend duty. But she spent a lot of time driving the back roads of central Maine, where cellphone reception was iffy at best and a breakdown in mid-winter could have serious consequences. Her dad's other prized possession, a restored early fifties Chris Craft U-22, a beautiful 22-foot wooden inboard, had been left to one of her older brothers. He had promised a while back to give it to her, but recently reneged, claiming that his kids wouldn't let him part with it. The boathouse she had renovated in anticipation of housing a treasured memory of her youth now stood empty, a hollow reminder of what she had left behind.

A squall line was moving toward her and Anne slowed in anticipation, reminding herself again that she needed a new set of tires. As the rain hit, her thoughts turned to the weather and to the coming winter. Even though it was months away there were reminders everywhere that winter was coming – the steadily growing stacks of cut and split firewood she saw next to beat-up trailers sitting on blocks in small clearings in the forest, the plastic rods sticking up from fire hydrants that would mark their location under snow banks, the rusted snowplows offered for sale along the roadside. Anne had enjoyed the winters in Michigan but winters in central Maine seemed qualitatively different – longer, darker, more depressing, with signs of poverty and hard times everywhere. Just last week, as she opened the front door of the True-Value Hardware in downtown Dover-Foxcroft she had seen a small handwritten sign posted in the window – "Kidney wanted" and a phone number. Next to it was an announcement of a fundraiser dinner for a local woman with mounting hospital bills from a tree branch that had pierced her windshield and bored into her head.

Along with the brutal winters and the crushing poverty that Anne had seen too much of down the back roads of Piscataquis County, she was also getting worn down by the day to day grind of responding to domestic violence calls, petty thefts, drug busts and bar fights, along with drunken snowmobilers and ATV accidents – a seemingly endless stream of sadness and wasted lives. It hadn't seemed so bad when she first started. Anne and George McCormick, the Piscataquis County Sherriff who hired her, had hit it off from the start and he had supported and encouraged her, even teaming her up with Doug Bateman on a high profile serial murder case soon after she first arrived. But when McCormick retired, Charles Hudson had won election, and he was making life miserable for Anne - ridiculing her in public, assigning her all the low-importance complaints, and throwing in a lot of sexual harassment along the way. She had kept her mouth shut so far, and endured the treatment, but her self-respect was being worn down and there didn't appear to be an easy solution in sight.

And then there was the lingering puzzle of Doug Bateman. He and Anne had formed a close working relationship during the long hours they had spent together tracking a serial killer a few years back. Anne had hoped it would develop into something more and thought that Doug shared her feelings. He had been estranged from his wife Beth at the time, and there was talk of divorce around town. But Beth had moved back in with Doug, and from all accounts they were trying to work out the problems in their marriage. Beth was commuting down to Orono every day where she was managing a coffee shop and café close to the University of Maine campus. Anne hadn't had much contact with Doug since the previous fall, but still thought about him far too frequently.

Taking the route 11 exit off the interstate, Anne called the Penobscot County Sheriff's office to let them know that she was responding to their request for Piscataquis County to look into the burglary at the Patten Lumberman's Museum and was surprised to learn that she had her facts backward. They hadn't called Sheriff Hudson asking for help – he had somehow learned of the robbery and had called them and asked if one of his junior investigators could take over the case – that she needed the experience.

As Anne walked in the front door to the museum she was ready to take a quick report of the break-in – it should take fifteen minutes tops - and then she could head back to Dover-Foxcroft to have it out with Hudson. Maybe the best thing to do was just to tell him to shove the job, pull up stakes, and head back to the Midwest.

Two hours later, Anne headed south out of Patten. Rather than getting a quick report on the theft she had ended up taking a guided tour of the museum's various buildings and exhibits. Anne was aware that lumbering had played an important role in the economy of Maine for more than a century and a half, but she really hadn't appreciated what was involved in the harvesting and transport of timber down Maine's rivers to the mills. The museum brought the harsh lives of Maine's early lumbermen to life for her: the demanding and dangerous work deep in the forests; the long lean-to like structures they crowded into during the sub-zero winter nights, twenty men sleeping side by side, kept warm by cook fires and the body heat of the draft animals that shared the space; the challenge of moving the logs downstream with the spring thaw, dancing across rafts of thousands of logs moving in swift currents, where with a single miss-step a lumberman could vanish into the cold dark depths.

As Anne placed the photographs and descriptions of the two axes that had been removed from one of the museum's exhibits on the passenger seat of her Toyota, along with several books she had bought, she smiled as she realized that she should probably thank Sheriff Hudson for assigning her to the burglary. She had needed reminding of what a remarkable life she was living in this beautiful place, and the lumberman's museum had pulled her out of her dark mood. In addition, Hudson would be irritated if she thanked him for an assignment he had hoped would push her toward quitting. The storm had passed, the sun was out, and the trees along the interstate formed a glistening mosaic of greens.

Anne took the Route 155 exit off the Interstate and headed southwest toward Lagrange, where she would pick up Route 6 up to Milo and then west over to Dover-Foxcroft. Her phone rang just as she reached the intersection of Routes 155 and 6 at Lagrange, and she pulled off the road into the shade of a large maple tree. It was Doug Bateman.

"Hi Doug," Anne answered. "What can I do for you?"

"Anne, it's good to hear your voice. Got some good news for you. We found one of your stolen axes."

"What? Where? How did you know it was my case?"

"We sent some photos up to the Patten Lumberman's Museum. I just got off the phone with the curator up there. She confirmed it was one of the axes taken from their exhibits, and that you were investigating the case."

"Where did you find it?"

"It was embedded in the head of a murder victim discovered up on Sugar Island on Sunday."

"The Richard Potter killing?"

"Right. If McCormick was still sheriff I am sure that he would agree that the cases were connected, and have you join the murder investigation. But this new guy Hudson has already refused my request to have you assigned to the Potter case. He sounds like a real piece of work."

Anne paused, surprised, before responding

"You asked for me?"

"I did. I made the request before we knew about the axe, but I doubt he will change his mind now. My guess is that smart, competent people threaten him and that he wants to keep you busy working on minor stuff, even if it involves sending you outside the county. I was thinking that maybe we could compare notes informally? We could really use your input on the Potter case."

Smiling broadly now and thrusting her fist in the air, while trying to sound calm and collected, Anne responded.

"I think I might be able to manage that Doug. I'm working on a rape case right now but could carve out some time. Hudson's head would explode if he found out though, so we would have to be careful."

"That's great Anne. How about breakfast at Spencer's on Friday – eight o'clock?

Anne paused again before replying and decided that she wasn't going to worry about what Sheriff Hudson might think if he heard about the breakfast with Doug.

"That should work."

"Excellent," Doug responded.

As Anne ended the call, she noticed a late model gray SUV, maybe a Chevy Suburban, pull into the parking lot of the Lagrange store on the southwest corner of the intersection. It had dark tinted windows and Massachusetts plates and sat idling as if waiting for someone. Her curiosity piqued, Anne figured she could give it ten minutes or so and see what happened. Just as she was about to give up and pull out onto the highway, a red Toyota FJ Cruiser pulled up alongside the SUV, and the drivers of both vehicles began a conversation through their open driver-side windows. Anne slid down in her seat, reached over for her binoculars, and wrote down the license number of the SUV. She still could not see the driver of the Suburban, but had no difficulty identifying the red FJ and its driver – it was the Piscataquis County Sheriff, Charlie Hudson. After about five minutes Hudson turned around and headed back toward Milo. As Hudson disappeared down Route 6 the driver of the SUV got out and walked toward the Lagrange store, emerging a few minutes later with a coke and bag of Fox potato chips. Short, burley, in his mid-forties, with dark hair cut short, wearing jeans and a sweatshirt, he was not someone Anne recognized. Feeling a little silly, she snapped a few photos of the mystery man with her phone.

When Anne was back in her office she first called the Patten Lumberman's Museum to let them know she had been in contact with Detective Bateman regarding the recovery of the museum's axe, and that she would be in touch when she knew when they would get it back. Then turning to her other case, she logged into the FBI's Violent Criminal Apprehension Program (ViCap) web site and entered information about the Gayle Robertson rape. Even though Anne was aware that only a small percentage of law enforcement agencies across the country participated in the system and less than one percent of the violent crimes committed each year were entered into ViCap, she still thought it was worth the effort, given the unusual nature of the rape. She wasn't surprised when her subsequent search of the ViCap database for cases similar to the Robertson rape turned up nothing. FBI analysts would be reviewing her submitted report, she knew, and would be conducting a more in-depth search for other similar cases. If she got lucky maybe they would turn up something and contact her.

Looking up Gayle Robertson's contact information, Anne sent her an email asking if she remembered anything else – any unusual encounters in the weeks leading up to her attack, any strangers hanging around the neighborhood, any sense that someone was following her. Since the rape had occurred in her home, Anne then contacted her landlord for information and started working through the standard list of people who may have encountered her there, including her propane supplier, her garbage collection company, newspaper deliveries, any recent repairs to the house by local contractors, and internet and cable company installers. Her efforts didn't turn up anything of interest until her final call. She checked with Fran Waybridge at the Dover-Foxcroft Post Office, who turned the phone over to Joanne Jefferies, who was the delivery person who handled Gayle's area. Joanne said she did remember something unusual – a white pickup truck with Maine plates – the one with the loon on it – she didn't notice the plate numbers - was parked down the street from Gayle's house on several occasions in the week leading up to the attack. Joanne noticed the truck because it was idling both times and the man behind the wheel seemed to be just sitting there reading something on his lap. She described him as white, medium build, maybe a bit chunky, with longish dark hair. He had a baseball hat pulled down so Joanne couldn't get a good look at his face. Anne made a note to canvas the other houses on the street to see if anyone else had noticed the truck and its driver, and left for the day. Driving home she realized it wasn't much of a lead given the abundance of white pickup trucks in central Maine. As she passed the Bear's Den restaurant Cowboy pulled his white pickup out of the parking lot and followed her at a safe distance.

8.
COWBOY
FRIDAY

It was a clear moonless night and Jimmy Bob Lentz was in a contemplative mood. Sitting on the front porch swing of Becky Crawford's house in Milo, humming to himself and rocking back and forth quietly so as not to wake her, he wondered what his next name would be. He liked "Jimmy Bob" – it reminded him of his west Texas roots, but he had used it for almost six months now and figured he would get a new one when he left Maine. He had grown to like central Maine – the vast stretches of forest broken only by winding two-lane highways, swiftly flowing streams, and pristine lakes and ponds – so different from the harsh landscapes of west Texas and New Mexico he had known growing up. But he was glad this was a short-term assignment, and that it was summer – he wouldn't want to have to spend a winter here, and wondered how the locals survived.

Jimmy Bob had been to many different parts of the country over the past decade and his identity had been changed every few times he relocated. It was easy now, really – once an assignment was completed he would be directed to where to pick up a new identity packet and instructions for his next job, and deposits into his bank accounts were always on time. For the first few years his relocations to new assignments and the shedding of old identities had often been complicated and cumbersome, but the Mercedes Airstream had made the transitions much easier. Now he had a permanent home that went with him when he relocated. Taking on new identities didn't bother the man humming and swinging on Becky's front porch swing, since he didn't have a real name, or at least he had never learned it.

He was probably about twelve years old when Abraham Lentz had pulled up beside him as he walked by the side of a West Texas back road in on a cold windy day in February. Stopping his car, Lentz had briefly gazed at him with a calculating expression and told him to get in the car. He climbed in the front seat – men always rode up front, he would learn, and was immediately enveloped in the warm embrace of the Waldo Christian Family of Heaven and Earth.

Abraham, the Patriarch of the Family, asked him his name, and when he said he didn't have a name, the Patriarch looked in the rearview mirror, smiled, and pronounced:

"Like Moses in the second chapter of Exodus, you have been rescued from the wilderness and adopted into the royal family of heaven on earth. We shall call you Enoch – the dedicated one."

"Praised be his presence among us," was the response from the back seat, and the newly named Enoch turned to take a closer look at the three women in identical ivory dresses and headscarves smiling at him and nodding in unison. They were an unusual trio – the one in the middle was short, overweight, with a wandering eye, and looked to be in her forties. The women on either side were younger, taller, rail thin, and might have been twins. All three were plain, devoid of makeup, with their hands chastely folded in their laps.

The Patriarch put the car in gear, and gazing over at Enoch, he noticed the cluster of raw wounds on the back of his left hand.

"How did you get those marks on your hand, boy?"

"A cigar."

"Who did that to you?"

"A man."

"That all you got to say about it, boy?"

Enoch nodded, and after a long pause, the Patriarch responded.

"Well, that's all behind you Enoch. That life is in the past. You have been reborn into a loving family right here on the road to Damascus and we shall cherish you and nurture you and you shall,

God willing, produce a multitude of sons and daughters for the growing Christian community of Waldo." A joyful chorus of "Praised be his presence among us," came from the back seat, followed by raucous giggles and good-natured elbowing.

In the quiet early morning darkness of Willow Street in Milo, Maine, Jimmy Bob Lentz smiled to himself as he remembered the early years in Waldo, before things went bad, and how the twins and Faith, the walleyed one, had indeed taught him what he needed to know. Late that afternoon he had watched Becky's housemate Heather drive off for a planned weekend with her boyfriend over on the coast, and he was confident that he and his new bride would not be disturbed. Now and then a car could be heard up on Pleasant Street, but with the exception of an occasional tomcat yowl, Becky's street was quiet. It was around four in the morning and Jimmy Bob was just about ready to wake Becky and begin the marriage ceremony. His backpack was open so he could get quick access to zip ties and a blindfold, and he had added a small tape recorder to his kit. He thought it would be nice to play a recording of the marriage vows – to make the occasion more romantic and memorable. The front door key, which Jimmy Bob had retrieved from its hiding place, was in his right hand, and he held his Dundee Style Bowie Knife loosely in his left hand. On the porch swing next to him was a bouquet of fresh wildflowers he had picked earlier in the evening from a meadow along the road over from Dover-Foxcroft. Jimmy Bob was a romantic at heart.

Getting up from the swing he pulled on his latex gloves, picked up the flowers in his knife hand, and silently entered the house. Locking the front door behind him he set the front door key down on the living room coffee table and moved to Becky's bedroom door, which was open. Stepping quietly to her bedside he called her name as he shined the LED flashlight into her face from a few feet away. Becky started to sit up and opened her mouth to scream. Jimmy Bob showed her the knife and quickly placed it against her throat as he whispered to her to shut up. Once her blindfold was in place and taped, he added a strip of tape over her mouth. He continued to talk to her in a calm, soothing voice as he ziptied her hands and attached them to the bed frame above her head.

"Don't be scared Becky – I'm not going to hurt you. I think you're a wonderful young woman of good character, and I applaud your decision not to have intimate relations until you're married."

Once Becky was secured, Jimmy Bob placed the flowers on the bed next to her.

"I brought you some flowers and hope that you will accept my offer of marriage."

Becky was rigid with fear and started to quietly sob behind the gag.

"Becky, pay attention." He placed the flat of the knife blade against her neck as he whispered to her. "Will you marry me? You can just nod your head yes."

She nodded quickly and Jimmy Bob slid the knife off her neck and used it to cut the buttons off her pajama top, exposing her breasts and eliciting a new round of sobbing, louder this time. After dropping one of the buttons into his backpack – to add to his collection of wedding souvenirs, he pulled her pajama bottoms off and paused to take several photos for the wedding scrapbook, making sure that the bouquet of flowers was included in the shots. Reaching over Becky, Jimmy Bob selected one of the prettier flowers and slipped it into the backpack – he could press it and include it in the scrapbook.

Fishing the tape recorder out of his pocket, he placed it on the bed.

"Becky, I am going to remove your gag now and play a recording I made of the marriage ceremony. When the time comes, you will need to respond 'I do.' If you don't say it, or if you cry out, I will cut you. Understood?"

Becky nodded again and Jimmy Bob ripped off the tape over her mouth. She gasped in pain and then froze in fear. Jimmy Bob started the tape recorder and against a soft background of organ music, the ceremony began.

"Dearly beloved, we have come together in the presence of God to witness and bless the joining together..."

Becky whispered "I do" at the appropriate time and when the ceremony ended Jimmy Bob drew a small velvet box out of his pack and reaching up, slipped the wedding ring that had consecrated so many of his previous marriages onto Becky's left-hand ring finger. Cradling her head in his hands gently but firmly, Jimmy Bob kissed her on the lips before taping a fresh length of tape over her mouth.

"Wasn't that a nice ceremony Becky? Did you like it? We're going to have a wonderful life together and our wedding night is going to produce a fine healthy baby."

Becky went rigid with fear as Jimmy Bob loosened the gag just far enough to slip a ketamine capsule into her mouth.

"Swallow the pill Becky. It will help you to relax while I put the baby."

Jimmy Bob sat by Becky's side and talked to her about his dreams for their future together until, after ten minutes or so, the drug took effect. He was expecting some level of struggle or agitation from his new bride as he joined her in bed, but she simply closed her eyes and lost consciousness.

Once he had consummated his marriage to Becky, Jimmy Bob heated up his branding iron on the kitchen stove and seared the numeral "10" into her right haunch. Becky had no reaction to the branding as the smell of burning flesh filled her bedroom. Jimmy Bob removed the wedding ring, repacked his backpack, and checked to make sure he wasn't leaving anything behind. Stepping out onto the front porch, he left the front door unlocked. He was concerned about Becky – her pulse when he checked was rapid and her breathing was shallow. Deciding to take no chances with her health and the health of the baby, he called 911, using Becky's phone.

"911. What is your emergency?"

"A woman has been assaulted and needs medical attention."

"What is your location?"

"65 Willow Street in Milo. Hurry, please."

As the operator asked him to identify himself Jimmy Bob hung up the phone and placed it on the porch swing. Removing his latex gloves, he walked quickly away from the house and cut through the neighboring yard and then made his way down to the parking lot for Elaine's Bakery and Café, where he had left his truck. Elaine's was Jimmy Bob's favorite place for breakfast – he was addicted to the donuts but he was careful to not eat at any one place too often. Many of his meals were from the McDonalds or Dunkin Donuts out by the Shaw's Supermarket in Dover-Foxcroft or from the Swift Creek BBQ in Monson or Auntie M's in Greenville – places where the staff was constantly changing and constantly busy – and less likely to remember him. He also liked the sandwiches and other ready to eat items for sale at Shaw's.

Dropping his backpack in the truck Jimmy Bob entered Elaine's by the side door off the deck, taking a seat at a table by the front window that offered a clear view of downtown Milo. As he sat down he noticed a Milo Police cruiser with its light bar flashing as it turned the corner and accelerated up the hill on Pleasant Street toward Becky's house. "That was fast," he thought, and ordered a coffee and a traditional cake donut. Jimmy Bob decided a celebration was in order – a wedding breakfast of sorts, and ordered the Scrambler. As he was paying his bill at the counter an EMT vehicle, siren blaring, turned the corner and climbed the hill up toward Becky's.

Settling in behind the steering wheel of his truck he waited for the ETM truck to return, and when it did he waited until it had crossed the dam before pulling out behind it and following at a safe distance. The EMT truck carrying Becky was not being escorted by the police cruiser and neither its light bar nor siren were on, indicating that Becky was not in any danger. Jimmy Bob figured the ambulance must be taking Becky over to the Mayo Regional Hospital in Dover-Foxcroft, and since it was on his way home he might as well follow and see if he could get a glimpse of her when she was moved from the ambulance into the hospital. When they got closer to

Dover-Foxcroft Jimmy Bob passed the ambulance so he could arrive at the Mayo Hospital before it did and find a good parking place to observe the patient transfer. He found an excellent vantage point, parked the truck, and watched Becky being wheeled into the hospital on a gurney. She looked to be conscious and the EMT staff did not seem overly concerned. It looked like his bride and her baby were going to be OK.

Jimmy Bob pulled out of the hospital parking lot, and headed west out of town. As he passed Spencer's Bakery and Cafe he noticed Anne's green Toyota Land Cruiser, and caught a glimpse of her through the window, sitting in one of the booths.

"Wouldn't it be perfect if she was investigating the rapes?" he thought to himself – "the investigator looking into my marriages can herself become one of my brides." Smiling broadly, Jimmy Bob headed home.

It had been a long night, and after a quick shower and a restorative nap, Jimmy Bob put his wedding night kit away, downloaded his photos of Becky, and added the button and flower to his collection of memorabilia. He finalized their wedding announcement, adding in the additional information about Becky and her family he had gleaned from his web searches, and completed his "#10 Becky" file in the "Marriages" folder on his computer.

Shifting over into his prospective brides folder, Jimmy Bob opened the Anne Quinn file and started working on a wedding announcement. Both of Anne's parents had passed away but he worked her two older brothers into his narrative and was pleased with his initial draft. He added the photos he had taken of Anne over the past four days with his long lens, including several he had caught of her riding her bike one morning along a country road outside of town. He was continuing to be careful in his tracking of Investigator Quinn, making sure to not get too close, particularly when he was in the truck, and taking photos only from a distance. She would be much more likely to notice that she was being followed than his other brides. After another hour of surfing the web in search of information about Quinn and photos of various aspects of her life, Jimmy Bob realized that he might be getting dangerously obsessed with this woman. If he was going to claim her as his bride he would need to be very cautious, very methodical, and to plan the wedding night with extra care.

9.
DOUGLAS
FRIDAY

Doug slid into the booth across from Anne Quinn at Spencer's Café in Dover-Foxcroft at about 8:15, just as Jimmy Bob drove by and noticed Anne's Land Cruiser in the parking lot. It was crowded, as usual, during the breakfast rush hour, but Kate Bishop, one of the harried waitresses, and a regular at Anne's informal practices for Foxcroft Academy's Lady Ponies girls basketball team, came right over with a big smile, menus, and coffee. It was clear to both Doug and Anne that Kate would no doubt be reporting on their breakfast meeting via social media as soon as they left, if not sooner.

Doug had thought a lot about how to start this conversation – he knew that Anne was justifiably hurt by the way he had suddenly stopped all contact with her after the murder case they had worked on together had ended. One look at her stony expression convinced him that his planned opening gambit – a joking reference to their shared obsession with donuts from Elaine's Bakery over in Milo, wasn't going to work. He decided to skip the small talk.

"So what do you think it will take to get Sheriff Hudson to detail you over to the Rick Potter murder investigation?" Doug asked. "He turned me down when I asked a week ago. But now we know that axe taken during the break-in at the Lumberman's museum was the murder weapon, and Hudson said if the cases were linked he would assign you to the murder. Will he keep his word do you think? What's the best way to approach him?"

Doug waited for Anne's reply. During her playing days as point guard for the University of Michigan women's basketball team Anne was known for her aggressive drives to the basket, and she decided that's what was called for here.

"So all this time, all these months, Doug, not a word from you. Nothing. Then out of the blue, it's 'Hey, how ya been? Maybe we should work together again.'"

Doug saw the anger and hurt on her face, and quietly responded.

"Beth insisted that I break off any communication."

Anne said nothing, just sat back in the booth and waited. Doug was about to continue when Kate Bishop materialized at his elbow; hoping to overhear what looked like it was going to be a good interchange. Once they had ordered breakfast, and Kate had reluctantly drifted away, Doug continued.

"That was one of Beth's conditions for moving back in and working on our marriage – that I not have any contact with you at all. She considered you a 'disruptive influence'."

Anne smiled at the characterization but remained silent, and Doug forged ahead.

"I'm sorry Anne. It was a mistake. I never should have agreed, but I thought I owed it to our marriage to try to work things out with Beth."

Anne took a sip of her coffee, set the cup down, and casually asked the question.

"So how are things going with you and Beth?"

"Beth's pregnant."

Anne couldn't hide her surprise, both at the announcement of Beth's pregnancy and at Doug's seemingly nonchalant attitude. Puzzled, Anne's response came out forced and insincere.

"Congratulations. You both must be very pleased."

Doug shrugged, looked directly at her, and replied.

"It's not mine."

"Not yours? So... what does that mean?"

"It's over. Beth left town a few days ago – has lined up a job in Santa Fe, is moving out there with the child's father. I'll file for divorce – uncontested. So in a few months I'll be unmarried."

"You don't seem upset."

"I'm not. Maybe still a little confused, but mostly just relieved. I don't think Beth was ever really happy with the marriage or with me. She was always angry and disappointed – wanting more. It's weird, really - not having to worry about what kind of a mood she's in anymore."

Doug was about to say more when Kate showed up with the bill. Doug's phone rang and after listening briefly, he responded "I'm on my way," and ended the call. Standing up from the booth he moved to the counter to pay the bill, motioning to Anne to follow him. When they stepped outside, Doug scanned the parking lot before turning to Anne.

"Another body's been found - up at Kokajo – axe to the head. It could be the second axe from the Patten Lumberman's Museum. Can you come with me to the scene?"

Anne shook her head.

"I can't. Hudson would fire me. You'd have to clear it with him first."

Doug nodded, reached out, gently pulled her to him, and kissed her on the lips. Stepping back, he smiled and asked if she would be at the fundraising event at Central Hall that evening. Anne nodded, somewhat bemused, and Doug laughed, pleased to have surprised her.

"See you there."

Inside Spencer's Café, Kate Bishop was standing behind the cash register, frozen in place, her mouth hanging open.

"Oh. My. God." she whispered to herself. "Doug Bateman just kissed Anne. He just kissed her in the parking lot." She reached for her phone and began texting rapidly.

Doug pulled the blue police flasher up from the floor of the jeep, turned it on, and placed it on the dash for the trip over to Greenville. He made good time as the vehicles he overtook pulled over for him to pass, including Jimmy Bob's white pickup truck a little north of the town of Shirley. When Doug reached Greenville he continued up along the east side of Moosehead Lake on Lily Bay Road, passing Northwoods Outfitters, the Shaw Public Library, and Auntie M's Restaurant on the way out of town. It took him another half hour to reach Kokajo. Boasting a general store and a population of "not many," Kokajo was situated at the west end of First Roach Pond and marked the end of paved roads. North of it stretched a vast wilderness of crisscrossing logging roads and scattered remote fishing and hunting camps.

Doug slowed at the curve south of Kokajo and pulled over behind a Greenville Police SUV that was parked next to a large hand-painted billboard that read "Keep Maine Green. This is God's country. Why set it on fire and make it look like hell?" A Greenville police officer was leaning up against the billboard and Doug could see yellow crime scene tape stretched into the woods behind it. Showing his ID and signing the crime scene log, Doug stepped around the corner of the billboard and joined Chief Marcus and another of his officers.

Shaking Doug's hand, Marcus pointed back into the woods.

"You can see the body back through the trees. We haven't gone any closer – just taped it off until the Evidence Response Team can check it out."

Doug peered back into the woods in the direction the chief had pointed.

"I called Peter Martell first thing chief, and they are on their way. Should be here in an hour or so. Meantime let's mark a trail over to the body with some tape. As long as we stay close to it we shouldn't disturb much in the way of evidence."

Doug and Chief Marcus approached within about ten feet of the corpse, which was close enough, given the smell of decomposing flesh and the maggots actively feeding in the multiple wounds they could see.

"Looks like it's been here two or three days," Doug estimated. "Who discovered it?"

"Two teens from Kokajo, twins – Shaw and Hope Walker, smelled it when they walked passed the billboard and went to investigate.

They saw it well enough when they rounded the billboard to figure out what it was and didn't go any closer. The call came in from the general store in Kokajo. We questioned the twins and then let them go."

Doug nodded and replied.

"Adult female, tied to a tree, axe still embedded in the back of her head – similar to the Richard Potter murder but not identical. Could be the same killer but there are some differences. The axe is definitely not the second axe taken from the lumberman's museum. This one is a double-bitted axe – maybe Wisconsin or Michigan pattern, and it has a name written on the handle. It's worn down quite a bit, but I would guess it says 'Merrill.' The Merrill's were a big timbering dynasty in this part of Maine. We need to follow up on that. And the wounds are different – no killing blow at the nape of the neck, but a number of wounds on the victim's back, both blunt trauma and gashes – looks like both the blade and side of the axe head may have been used. The lack of bleeding from any of the wounds, including the head wound indicates, I would guess, that the killing occurred elsewhere. So we need to be careful to preserve any tire tracks or footprints. Let's extend the perimeter to include the shoulder of the road in both directions for fifty yards or so."

Returning to the pavement, Chief Marcus and Doug watched the two officers tape off the shoulders of the road and talked over the progress, or lack thereof, on the Richard Potter case as they waited for the Evidence Response Team to arrive.

"Well, we've followed up on a lot of leads, Doug, but turned up nothing. John Shea, the malcontent from the town hall meeting, has an alibi for all day Sunday, as do most of the other people with an axe to grind with Potter." Marcus smiled at his turn of phrase before continuing. "We're still looking for the second axe – the divers are back out at Sugar Island this afternoon."

Doug nodded and responded.

"The big question now is whether the two murders are linked. Is it the same killer, or do we have a copycat killing? If the victim here was at the town hall meeting and was opposed to the Lily Bay project, that will certainly strengthen the likelihood that it's a single killer and strongly suggest a motive."

Once the Evidence Response Team arrived and began to process the scene Chief Marcus and Doug had to wait another half hour before they were allowed back behind the billboard. Peter Martell briefed them on what they had learned.

"We have a good outline of what happened here – no rain this time and little disturbance of the scene. It looks like the victim was killed somewhere else and transported here based on the lack of blood, the nature of the wounds, and evidence on the ground. There's a good set of tire tracks pulling off the pavement about 30 yards south of the billboard, coming from the direction of Greenville. We've got shoeprints leading from the driver's side back to the rear of the vehicle and then over to the tree where the victim was tied, along with drag marks where the body was pulled, and corresponding lacerations, scuffing and dirt on the victim's heels and lower body. So if you get a vehicle or footwear we can make a match."

"What about the wounds?" Doug asked.

"Cause of death, which happened somewhere else, looks to be a single stab wound to the chest – a big knife, probably dead center on the heart."

"What about the other wounds on the back?"

Leading Chief Marcus and Doug over to the body, Martell continued.

"It looks like the killer tied the victim to the tree in the tree hugger position and then practiced his axe throwing. You can see where he walked back and forth maybe a dozen times. He wasn't very good – mostly he hit the victim with the poll or handle of the axe, with the blade cutting into the victim only two or three times. It might be significant that he threw from about 20 feet away, which is the standard distance for axe throwing competitions. So maybe he's an axe-throwing enthusiast. If so, he's not very accomplished."

"And then, after he's done with the throwing, he goes for the head?"

"Right. A single stroke to the back of the skull."

"What about the victim – any indications of identity?"

Martell shook his head as Chief Marcus bent down and looked at the face of the dead woman before answering Doug's question.

"I know who it is – should have identified her sooner. It's Virginia Breen. She's one of the wealthiest women in the state – or was, I should say. A real piece of work – a knockout when she was younger, but she put on a lot of weight in the last decade – early forties I think. Breen has had lots of issues with alcohol and pills – in rehab off and on. I can think of at least a half dozen people who would be happy to see her dead – so we have no lack of suspects. She's a major landowner in central and northern Maine and owns a lot of real estate down on the coast – big into timber harvesting and high-end resort development. Very litigious – her hobby is taking state and local governments and business competitors to court and fighting over property development and resource extraction regulations and contracts. She's a real bitch."

Looking for a possible link to the Potter killing, Doug asked if Breen had been at the town hall meeting on the development plans for Lily Bay.

"Yes – she was definitely there and spoke out against it. Not because she was concerned about the environment or the impact of the development, but because it wasn't her development. I also think that she has an active case in court against Richard Potter for some property issue."

"O.K." Doug replied. "We need to notify her family of her death and interview them about her recent movements and any disputes that might have flared up over the last month or so."

Chief Marcus nodded. "We can handle that Doug, and can also start working up a list of her adversaries and their possible motives for you."

Bateman, Marcus and Martell walked back out to the road just as a hearse from the local funeral home arrived to transport the body down to Augusta for autopsy. Doug and Chief Marcus headed back down to Greenville, and Doug decided to drop in at the Kamp Kamp Indian Store to see if Randy and Cheri might have any leads on the double bit axe with 'Merrill' written on the handle. It looked to be a vintage axe – probably dating back to the 1930s or earlier, and a lot of vintage items, including axes, saws, and other tools associated with the lumbering industry passed through their hands. Randy maintained a large network of contacts throughout the state and worked both ends of the camp trade – being called in to look at old camps being sold or going through probate and selecting items to be recycled into new homes being built or renovated by his hunting camp and lake cabin customer base.

Skirting around the crowd of kids and their parents looking at tourist tchotchkes in the front room of the Kamp Kamp store, Doug found Cheri in her office staring at her computer screen, going over new orders. He had known her since he was a kid, and always enjoyed seeing her. Cheri was hard working, always moving, and always smiling and upbeat.

"How are things Cheri?"

"Oh, busy," Cheri replied, smiling up at Doug. "It was kinda slow last week with the rain but overall it's been a good summer so far. Can't complain. How about you? I hear you and Beth have split up. That's too bad, Doug. Someone else will come along." Patting Doug on the arm and moving quickly on from a sensitive topic, Cheri asked.

"Made any progress on the Little Rick murder?"

"Well Cheri, that's why I'm here. You'll hear soon enough – we have another killing with an axe, and I'm wondering if by any chance you've seen any double-bitted axes with 'Merrill' written on the handle."

"I don't think so Doug," Cheri replied, looking up from her computer. "But let's ask Randy – he's in the back room wrestling with an albino porcupine."

Walking through the curtained doorway into the back room,

Doug was once again mesmerized by the profusion of treasures that were crowded into the various alcoves and isles – taxidermied animals, snowshoes and skis, old signs, lamps, oars and paddles, fishing rods and lures, vintage clothing, dishes, chairs hanging from the rafters, rough camp furniture, primitive paintings, mounted fish.... Randy was in a back corner putting up a shelf for his newest find – a well mounted pure white porcupine with a price tag of $200. Doug laughed as he shook Randy's hand and then pointed at the porcupine.

"Randy, is someone really going to pay that much for that?"

"Doug, you would be amazed what people will pay good money for. Last year a couple from down your way, on Sebec Lake, paid fifty bucks for a snarling stuffed opossum. I had put it under a table way in the back because it was scaring the little kids and they pulled it out, got excited about what a good deal it was, and how good it would look in their camp. It didn't make any difference that we don't have opossums living around here – they liked that it was scary. Said they were going to name it Satan."

Doug shook his head and asked.

"We've got another axe murder and I'm trying to track down the murder weapon. Ever seen any double-bitted axes with 'Merrill' written on the handle?"

"A few over the years. We sold one here just a few weeks ago I think – I don't see it now and it was right over there in the corner with the other axes."

Turning to Cheri, Doug asked.

"Do you think you might have a receipt or credit card bill?"

"Probably not. I don't remember the sale, and we have a lot of people working for us during the busy season. We can check the CCTV footage though – we have a camera in the back room and I think it covers the axe corner. We can set it up for you – not sure how far back it goes, but we might get lucky."

It took several hours of looking, but Doug finally found the grainy footage of an average sized male with a slight limp and a large wide-brimmed hat, perfect for hiding his face from the camera, sorting through the axes. He hefted a double-bitted one with writing on the handle and then carried it out of view toward the front room and the cash register. Doug was about to turn off the recording when he noticed that the man had returned into view and walked back to the collection of axes in the corner. He sorted through them before picking up a second double-bitted axe and carrying both selections through the curtained doorway to the front of the store.

10.
ANNE
FRIDAY

Anne stood in the parking lot of Spencer's Bakery and Cafe and watched Doug's Jeep Cherokee turn west on route 6 toward Greenville. His announcement that his marriage to Beth was over, and then their very public kiss, had still not fully registered with her. Turning back toward the restaurant she saw Kate Bishop standing at the window, watching her while talking on her phone. Anne smiled at her, shrugging her shoulders, and Kate started jumping up and down. Wondering how long it would be before she got a call from her friend June Torben asking about her and Doug, Anne walked over to her vintage green Toyota Land Cruiser and started back to the office.

As she drove down Main Street, Anne felt a profound calmness settle over her. Douglas Bateman had been married for more than a decade and during their marriage she knew that Beth had not hesitated to let him know both how unhappy she was with their life – stuck in central Maine, and how disappointed she was in him. Given a chance – and they now had that chance, Anne was confident that she and Doug could build a lasting partnership. Things were definitely looking up. There was still a lot they had to discover about each other but Anne looked forward to a slow and easy development of their relationship. Driving over the Piscataquis River bridge between Foxcroft and Dover, she mused about what she might cook for their first dinner together – maybe her favorite - crab cakes, served on the dock of her south shore cabin, under the stars. Anne's cell phone rang, pulling her back from her daydream of crab cakes and candlelight, and she turned into the Center Theatre Coffee House parking lot to answer it.

"Hi Anne, it's Carol Merner at the Mayo – we just got another rape victim with a brand on her hip."

"I'm two minutes away, Carol. Meet me at the front door."

Carol led Anne back to a conference room. Once they were seated she slid a folder across the table to her.

"Her name's Becky Crawford. Here's the basic info we have so far. They brought her in early this morning by ambulance from her home in Milo. She had regained consciousness by the time she arrived but was still disoriented and pretty hysterical. We were able to get permission from her to do a full sexual assault forensic exam, but she has not told us much yet or agreed to be interviewed by law enforcement."

Opening the folder, Anne saw the photos of the brand - a "10" about the same size as the "9" that had been branded into the hip of Gayle Robertson, the first rape victim.

"Did she mention anything that you can tell me at this point?" Anne asked.

"Not really." Carol replied. "She was pretty out of it. She's sleeping now, and when she wakes up we'll ask again if she would be willing to talk to you. You'll want to review the 911 recording, though – someone called in on Becky's phone to report a medical emergency – it could have been her assailant."

Closing the file Anne thanked Carol, and as they walked back to the front entrance of the hospital Carol promised to update her on Becky Crawford's status later in the day. Arriving back at the sheriff's office Anne retrieved the 911 call and listened to it several times – no effort to disguise the voice, clearly a male, but no discernible regional accent or distinctive word choice. It would be useful for a voice comparison once they had identified a suspect, but first they had to find one.

Logging into the National Crime Database of the FBI's Violent Criminal Apprehension Program (ViCAP), Anne entered in the information she had so far for the Becky Crawford assault and checked again to see if she had received any responses to her previous entry on the web site of the attack on Gayle Robertson, either by an FBI analyst or other law enforcement personnel with similar cases across the country. Nothing new had been posted, which didn't surprise her, as data entry was cumbersome and she knew that participation in the system nation-wide was very low. Of the 80,000 forcible rapes and 14,000 homicides that occurred in 2013, for example, only a few hundred had been entered into ViCAP. Even so, Anne hoped that given the distinctive victim branding and the odd behavior of the assailant, information on previous similar crimes might have been entered.

Shortly after returning from lunch Anne's cell phone rang, listing a number she didn't recognize with a 703 area code.

"This is Anne Quinn."

"Investigator Quinn, my name is Patricia Crown. I'm calling from the FBI's National Center for the Analysis of Violent Crime here at Quantico. I'm an agent with Behavioral Analysis Unit Four – we monitor postings on ViCAP. I saw your recent entries for the two rapes in central Maine and wanted to let you know I'm starting a search of other available databases on a national scale to see what pops up. I have a vague memory of other scattered cases of rape involving branding or other forms of ownership marking being reported – it may be the same perpetrator."

"That's encouraging news Agent Crown – any help you can provide would be greatly appreciated. We have nothing to go on here except for a possible sighting of a white male in a white pickup truck close to the first assault. Any suggestions what we should look for?"

"Please, call me Patty. Well, actually, your entry describing the first rape, the Gayle Robertson assault, provides some good indicators. Let's give your perp the nickname 'Cowboy,' based on his signature – the branding of his victims. I'll be looking for branding, ear notching, and other forms of ownership marking commonly used in animal husbandry when I search the databases and reach out to law enforcement across the country. Cowboy fits the general profile of a serial rapist in several regards. He kidnaps his victims 'in place' you could say – restraining them and controlling them for an extended period of time. His gagging, binding, and blindfolding also fits the general pattern of serial rapists. Like serial rapists in general, Cowboy also uses verbal and physical threats – the choking, and he threatens the use of weapons – in his case a large knife. Drugging of the victims by serial rapists is also not uncommon, with Ketamine often the drug of choice.

Based on serial rapists in general, it's also highly likely that Cowboy's victims are not chosen at random – he searches them out and targets them, looking for women who fit a particular profile. Judging from what you've said he seems fixated on young women who are opposed to abortion and would be more likely to actually give birth to his baby, so that's the target group I would focus on. He might find his victims through direct person-to-person contact in social gathering places – anti-abortion demonstrations, community or church gatherings. Or he can be trolling online – Christian oriented dating sites, blogs and chat rooms. Once he identifies a potential target he will follow them for a period of time, learn their schedules and patterns of movement, and he may build profiles of them through online searches. Cowboy may also keep souvenirs – mementos, of his victims, and even some kind of scrapbook."

Rapidly taking notes as she listened to Agent Crown, Anne responded.

"So we're looking for a stalker. Cowboy's a hunter - a hunter with a clear idea of who his victims are. We can try to monitor his potential victim groups, looking for watchers on the margins, and also look for any indications of someone following women who fit his wish list – like the man in the white pickup truck."

"Yes," Patty responded. "And also – the obvious question – you have victims branded 9 and 10 – are there eight earlier victims, and are any of them there in central Maine? You should be looking statewide, and into Canada and neighboring states for any additional rapes with branding cases."

"I've done a statewide query, but not neighboring states or provinces, so I will do that today," Anne responded. "What do you think about the short time interval between the two rapes? Shouldn't there be more of a cooling off period?"

"That's a good point, Anne, and hard to explain. I would speculate that Cowboy has been busy building a list of potential victims and now is confronted with some sort of time constraint – he needs to work through his list before some deadline – it may be a perfectly logical deadline – maybe he has to leave the local area soon or it may be some sort of inexplicable personal psychological target date – the summer solstice, for example, or his mother's birthday. But you can't expect there to be much of a cooling off period. Cowboy will likely strike again soon."

"This is all a big help Patty. Anything more specific?"

"Yes. We don't have a lot to go on just yet, given only the single victim's account, and I hope that the second victim will agree to be interviewed and can fill in some blanks, but Gayle Robertson's account is actually quite revealing."

"In what way?"

"Well, serial rapists can be pretty typically sorted into one of four general categories, and Cowboy looks to fall comfortably into the last of these – called 'Power Reassurance.' Individuals in this category rape while being mildly aggressive, in order to restore their self-confidence. They have a sense of inadequacy, likely linked to their own past experience of physical or sexual abuse. They will often ask their victims for reassurance that they are good lovers, as Cowboy did with Gayle Robertson.

Given the Power Reassurance classification, it's also pretty safe to characterize Cowboy as passive, non-athletic, lacking in confidence, and incapable of having normal relationships with women. His effort to identify his victims as his fiancés and his strange marriage ceremony also fits the Power Reassurance classification – they often fantasize that the women they rape are their girlfriends."

"Pretty strange guy – I'm glad he's got a passive personality."

"Oh, I need to clarify that Anne. He presents a passive façade during the assaults, but he could be quite violent and unpredictable in other situations. Given his employment of the large knife and his choking and use of restraints, he should be considered very dangerous and approached with extreme caution. This is a very disturbed individual."

Before they ended the call, Agent Crown promised to be back in touch in a few days with any results from her search for other assaults involving branding or other ownership markings.

. . .

It was just past seven in downtown Dover-Foxcroft and the Friday evening reception celebrating the renovation of Central Hall, a landmark structure built in 1881, was well under way. Music and laughter spilled out of the front door as Doug Bateman walked up the newly laid brick walkway. Each brick carried the name of a contributor to the restoration fund for the historic building, which now had been returned to its former glory. Several people holding champagne flutes had wandered out of the reception to look for bricks with familiar names. Doug knew where the brick with his and Beth's name was located but had no interest in finding it.

He was looking forward to seeing Anne and inviting her to dinner after the reception. Dressed business casual in khakis and a dark blue Polo shirt, he entered the hall and scanned the clusters of people scattered around the large open common room, looking for Anne. A large group had gathered around Senator Susan Collins, who was scheduled to give a few remarks later, but Doug didn't see Anne. Grabbing a glass of champagne from a passing waiter, he joined June and Jim Torben, who were both looking uncomfortable as they struggled to make small talk with Charlie Hudson, the Sheriff of

Piscataquis County. Jim Torben had been promoted to Chief Deputy just before the previous sheriff had retired, and he had difficulty hiding his disdain for Hudson, a loud and obnoxious transplant from a Boston suburb. Raising his glass to the Torbens and Hudson, Doug turned to June.

"Have you seen Anne?"

"No Doug, I don't think she's arrived yet." June replied. Judging by her huge grin, Doug concluded that June, and probably half the town, had already heard of his breakfast meeting with Anne at Spencer's Café. Trying not to notice the food stains on the front of Sheriff Hudson's shirt, Doug smiled at him and was about to ask again about linking the murder cases with the theft of axes from the Patten Museum when Hudson anticipated his request.

"Don't even think about it Bateman. Investigator Quinn is fully engaged with her rape cases, and I have some other minor crimes I want her to investigate."

Hudson appeared about to continue, but he suddenly looked over Doug's shoulder toward the front door, pointed with his empty champagne glass, and blurted out:

"Jesus! Who's the fine piece of ass who just walked in?"

June frowned and turned to Doug.

"I'm not sure sheriff. Doug, do you know the woman?"

At first Doug didn't realize it was Anne. He was used to seeing her with her hair pulled back in a simple ponytail and dressed in work boots, faded flannel shirts and baggy jeans. Not tonight. Tonight she was transformed. She had stopped just inside the door and was looking around the room. Seeing Doug, she smiled. Slim, standing with an athlete's casual grace, she drew admiring glances from many of the men in the room. Her blond hair was pulled up in a simple chignon, exposing her long neck. A few tendrils had escaped and moved delicately in the soft breeze coming in the front door. Doug had never seen Anne wear makeup, but tonight she had applied a light lip-gloss and minimal eye shadow, setting off her blue eyes and the light scatter of freckles across her face. A sheer white silk sleeveless tuxedo shirt over a white camisole showed off her tanned, well-toned arms, and her black pencil skirt fell a few inches above her knees, showcasing long and shapely legs. The only jewelry she wore was a single strand of pearls and matching pearl stud earrings. Sleek, sophisticated, seeming transported from a different world, Anne radiated a warm glow of casual confidence and sensuality.

Frozen in place, Doug felt June poking him in the ribs and he was about to walk over to Anne when a tall redheaded man in a dark suit – someone he didn't recognize, blocked his view of her and handed her a glass of champagne. Taking her by the elbow the man led her over into a corner of the hall. Anne laughed at something he said to her, and they settled into an easy conversation. June leaned over and answered Doug's unasked question.

"That's Colin Watson. He's a Brit – owns a number of TV and radio stations in Maine and New Hampshire, and is apparently really rich. He comes all the way over to Dover-Foxcroft from Bangor most weekends to ride with Anne's cycling group. Word is he's sweet on Anne, and he's been chatting her up for the last few months. He's quite a catch I guess. I'm not surprised he came over for the reception - must have been lurking in the shadows waiting for her to arrive." Tongue in cheek she added "Don't you think they make a great couple?"

Draining his drink, Doug walked across the room toward Anne and Colin. As he joined them, Anne offered an enigmatic smile and Colin frowned at the intrusion.

"You look stunning tonight Anne."

"Thanks Doug. You clean up pretty well too. This is Colin Watson, over from Bangor for the evening. Colin, this is Doug Bateman with the State Police. He's investigating the recent murders up at Moosehead Lake."

Doug took in Colin's Saville Row suit, custom shirt, and expensive haircut, and took an immediate dislike to him, even before he spoke.

"Ah yes – Bateman – a common name in the UK - I imagine you have a lot of tenant farmers in your family tree. Do you till the soil, Mr. Bateman?"

Anne broke in before Doug could reply to the snide comment, hoping to deflect the conversation.

"Colin and I were just talking about cycling. He took it up in college back in England and has recently gotten back into it."

"Yes, that's right," Colin responded, keeping his eyes on Anne. A bunch of us at Oxford started a club of sorts – nothing official, but I enjoyed it. And I certainly enjoy riding with Anne – she is quite impressive."

Before Doug could respond, Colin reached over and grasped Anne's elbow.

"Mr. Bateman, very nice to meet you, but if you will excuse us I want to introduce Anne to Senator Collins."

Anne shrugged her shoulders and rolled her eyes at Doug as Colin led her away, signaling, "What can I do – she's a senator."

Over the next hour or so Doug stewed as he watched Colin shepherd Anne around from group to group, but he made no further attempt to talk to her. After Senator Collins had concluded her remarks, Doug got talking with his neighbor Kerry Israels about the recent deployment of the Bowerbank Volunteer Fire Department patio boat up to Tim's Cove, at the western end of Sebec Lake, to rescue a capsized sailboat. He didn't notice Jim Torben approach Anne and draw her away from a group of local dignitaries.

"Sorry for the interruption, Anne, I just wanted a quick word. I can't tell you much, and really shouldn't be saying anything – but I just wanted to give you a heads up that it's a good idea if you stay away from Sheriff Hudson – avoid dealing with him on anything as much as you can, just for the next few weeks. You didn't hear it from me but the Feds are interested in him as part of an investigation they have going."

Intrigued, Anne remembered the strange meeting of Hudson and the other man she had witnessed over at the Lagrange intersection.

"Let's go out to my car, Jim. I want to show you some photos I took earlier this week of Hudson meeting some sketchy guy over at Lagrange – just happened on them when I was coming back from Patten."

Jim whistled softly when he saw Anne's photos of the mystery man who had been talking to Hudson, and once she had texted him copies, he thanked her and hurried back into the hall, calling someone as he went.

Doug had looked up from his conversation with Kerry Israels just in time to catch a fleeting glimpse of Anne as she walked out the door with Jim Torben. He didn't get a good look at her companion and assumed the worst.

"Fuck me," he thought, "she just left with that Colin Watson prick."

A few minutes later he left the reception, which was winding down. Standing on the sidewalk, looking down Main Street toward the Bangor Savings Bank sign, Doug felt empty – defeated.

Hearing footsteps, he turned to see Anne approaching.

"Where's your Brit friend Colin?" Doug blurted out, sounding petulant.

Anne laughed softly as she came up close to him, her smiling face illuminated in the streetlight.

"Colin? He got angry and left a while ago. He invited me to join him on a trip to Paris he has coming up, and I declined. I told him I was involved with someone. Is that the truth Doug? Am I involved with someone?"

Still smarting, Doug replied.

"I'm not sure Anne. Not sure we have a future. After tonight I think maybe you're out of my league. You're a class act, I'm just a local Piscataquis County boy."

Anne looked at him with a suddenly serious expression, moved closer, and leaned up against him. He could feel the heat of her, could sense her body, her blue eyes, the blond tendrils framing her face.

"Doug, that's got to be the stupidest thing you've ever said. I'm convinced that we can build a great life together here in Piscataquis County." Leaning in, she kissed him.

11.
EMMA
FRIDAY

It was late Friday morning. Anne was at the courthouse in Dover-Foxcroft entering information into the FBI's ViCAP database. Doug was up at the Virginia Breen murder scene. Emma Lange was looking out the window of her room above the Black Frog restaurant at the people eating lunch on the dock. She still had trouble believing how her life had changed in less than a week. She had pitched her story idea to The Boston Globe on Wednesday after her interview with Detective Bateman and she got a call back the same afternoon requesting a story about the murder of Richard Potter. They wanted a first-person account of her lunch with him on the Sunday he was killed that included direct quotes from Potter on his opposition to the Lily Bay development. The editor she talked to also indicated that contingent upon reader response to her initial article, he would entertain the idea of a follow-up series of articles placing Potter's murder within the larger context of the planned Lily Bay development and its broader significance in the ongoing threats against the environment in northern New England. Emma quickly shelved her Thoreau project for the time being and had started to put the Potter piece together.

After ending the call with the Boston Globe editor, Emma had gone downstairs to the bar in the Black Frog where she cornered Jim Crocker, a Greenville policeman who was holding forth about the crime scene and the axe embedded in Potter's skull. He was reluctant to talk to her at first, even when she indicated he would be identified only as "a law enforcement officer on the scene," but opened up once she asked if he had perhaps been making up his account of what he had seen at the Potter camp on Sugar Island. Crocker pointed across the room to a pair of men having dinner who had also been present on Sunday afternoon, and both men confirmed his account and added additional details – the red twine around Potter's wrists, the blood pooled in his lower legs – "looked like he had waders on," and the dryness of the ground under the body that suggested he had been killed before the storm hit.

First thing Thursday morning Emma had met again with Sheriff Marcus, indicated she was writing an article for the Globe, and asked if he could provide an update on any progress on the case. Sitting behind his desk with his arms folded, Marcus was tightlipped, clearly irritated by the amount of information she had already found out.

"All I can tell you Miss Lange is that the case is still in its early stages. As you know, crimes of this nature are the responsibility of the State Police. The Greenville Police Department is cooperating fully with them in the investigation of the murder, but you will need to direct your questions to their public information office."

As soon as Emma left his office, Chief Marcus called Doug Bateman.

"Doug, wanted to give you a heads up. That Emma Lange woman was just in here – she's writing an article for the Boston Globe on the Potter murder. Sounds like she knows about as much as we do about the crime scene."

"Thanks chief, I will alert our public information people. Guess we will have to gird our loins for the press onslaught. Anything else developing there?"

"Not really. No new witnesses have come forward. I've got some local scuba guys going out tomorrow to search the shallows along the shore of Potter's camp – see if we can find the second axe."

Emma had worked on her article on the Potter killing for several hours Thursday, making sure to strengthen her chances of enticing the Globe to sign her up for a follow-up series by giving them what they were looking for. Potter was portrayed as a brave local environmentalist standing up to the powerful outside forces of rampant development, and Emma supported her characterization of him with carefully cherry-picked direct quotes. She sent the article off to the Globe early Thursday afternoon and it appeared online by dinner time, along with one of the photos she had taken of Potter at lunch, with his ornamented watch fob spread out on the table in front of him. By Friday morning she had heard back from the Globe editor. The article had drawn a lot of attention and had been picked up by other major print and online news organizations. She got the green light for up to three more follow-up articles spread over the next few weeks or so.

But soon after her article appeared Emma started getting a more detailed picture of Potter from a lot of different directions. Potter, it turned out, was a defender of the environment, but only when it suited his own ends. Just a few years ago he had closed off almost all recreational use of vast tracks of forest he had inherited - banning overnight camping, snowmobiles, ATVs, and hunting and fishing. He had also forced a number of long-term leaseholders on remote lakes within his lands to abandon their summer cabins and hunting camps. Unlike Roxanne Quimby of Bert's Bees, however, Potter's actions were not motivated by a desire to protect the environment, but rather were part of his own development plans – he wanted to create a series of small, remote, and exclusive high end fishing camps that featured all the amenities, catered to the rich, and could only be reached by float plane. The resultant resentment toward Potter was deep and enduring among local sportsmen and outdoor enthusiasts, not to mention the evicted leaseholders. Potter's camp on Sugar Island had been burglarized and his distinctive red Humvee had been the target of vandalism. Many of the insults hurled at him during the town hall meeting on the Lily Bay development plans had come from locals frustrated by Potter's closing off access to his lands.

It was not just the people who had been closed out of Potter's lands, however, who held a grudge against him. Many of the skilled tradesmen who had built remote luxury camps for him had been stiffed by Potter – paid far less than promised, if at all, and threatened with legal action when they pressed their claims. Potter was above all litigious – quick to file nuisance suits against anyone and everyone who objected to his plans.

The largest court fight he had been embroiled in when he was killed involved his efforts to block a planned development at Mt. Kineo, one of the major landmarks of Moosehead Lake. The dramatic 800-foot vertical cliffs of Mt. Kineo had formed the backdrop for a series of resort hotels, the first built in 1848. After the first two hotels at Kineo burned down in 1868 and 1882, the third reincarnation had, by 1911, expanded to accommodate more than 500 guests, and was the largest inland waterfront hotel in America. With the elimination of the railroad link in the 1930s and the collapse of the tourist trade, the hotel was scheduled for demolition and was destroyed by fire for a final time. All that remained at Kineo was a series of restored Victorian cottages along the water and a nine-hole golf course, the second oldest in New England, where players put their green fees in an honor system box in the small unattended "pro shop."

A real estate development company in Cincinnati had purchased a large parcel on the Kineo peninsula a few years back with plans to develop it as a planned community of several dozen summer homes. Potter had blocked the plans in court, not because he objected to the impact the proposed project would have on the scenic beauty of Mt. Kineo, but rather because he had his own plans for development in the area, which was close to his own home along the western shore of Moosehead Lake.

So while Potter had spoken out at the town hall meeting in opposition to the Lily Bay development it was not at all clear what his motivation had been, and Lily Bay backers were far from the only potential suspects in his killing. Emma's interviews of people in the Greenville and Moosehead Lake region over the next several days would include a number of individuals who had good reason to despise Potter, and she realized that the range of controversies he had been involved in provided a good format for her follow-up series of articles. Under the general heading of "Who killed Richard Potter?" she could outline the range of different disputes and adversaries that could have been involved in his murder, and at the same time address a number of broader issues that had shaped central and northern Maine's environmental debates for generations – what did ownership of land mean in the face of long-established traditions of open access and enjoyment? How were everyday people – local people, being denied use rights that had existed for hundreds of years? Who should get to decide what level of development and what kinds of development should be allowed and encouraged in order to both allow managed growth of communities and increased standards of living without erasing the long-standing fabric of community?

Struggling to figure out how she would structure her articles to tackle these larger themes, Emma was startled when a call from an unidentified number came in on her phone.

"Emma Lange, how's the research coming for your follow-up articles for the Globe? Potter was not exactly a pure-as-the-driven-snow tree hugger was he?"

"Who is this?"

"Oh. Sorry. My name is Fred Williams. I represent several parties who have taken an interest in your investigative reporting and your articles for the Globe. I'm having an early lunch here at the Black Frog and was hoping you might be able to take a break from your research and come down and join me. You haven't eaten yet have you?"

"How do you know where I am right now?

"You'd be surprised how much I know Emma. Just look out your window."

Emma glanced up from her computer and looked out the window. A man was sitting at a table for two out on the dock, holding a phone to his ear, and waving up at her. She paused, trying to decide whether to join the stranger.

"I can guarantee it will be worth your while Emma. And I hear the food here is pretty good – the Friday special is meatloaf."

Emma agreed, closed down her computer, and put the thumb drive that held all her notes and research in her pocket before heading downstairs to join Williams on the dock. Walking down the long hallway to the restaurant's entrance, past the long row of historical photographs from the first half of the twentieth century, Emma wondered who this guy was and what he wanted.

Williams stood up as she approached the table and smiled broadly – a smile that didn't extend to his eyes. He was of medium height, a little taller than Emma, probably in his mid-fifties, solidly built – muscular, with dark brown eyes and curly brown hair going gray at the temples. He was working hard at being charming, she could tell, but it didn't come easily. Judging from his expensive haircut, manicured nails, brightly polished tassel loafers, and Rolex watch, Williams was a man used to telling people what to do, and being obeyed. She noticed that his left ear was slightly cauliflowered due to blunt trauma of some form – maybe a wrestling or boxing injury. The tip of a tattoo – a rattlesnake tail? – was just visible on his left wrist below the cuff of his shirt. His handshake was firm and felt rough. He had the calloused fingers of someone used to manual labor.

"I hope I didn't disturb your writing Miss Lange – may I call you Emma?"

"You already have, Fred, but that's fine. What can I do for you?"

"Well, I just thought it might be a good idea for us to compare notes. I can understand why you pitched your first article the way you did – leaving the readers of the Globe with the impression that Potter was killed because of his righteous opposition to the dark forces behind the planned development at Lily Bay. It was a good way to get the Globe to sign on for another three articles."

Williams saw the surprise on Emma's face and smiled broadly again before continuing.

"But I would guess that you have begun to get a better picture of Potter and the people who had real reasons to kill him. He was no threat to the Lily Bay project – just a local gasbag with his own agenda. He has become more of an irritant dead than he ever was alive, thanks to your article."

Handing Emma a menu, Williams suggested they order. Emma opted for the Cheezy Weasel – the Black Frog's signature burger, and a side of curly fries. Williams settled for ice tea and a salad.

Emma decided to take back the initiative.

"Just exactly who are you Fred. What do you want?"

"I'll keep it simple. I can't really get into whom I represent – let's just say that they have the best interests of the local community at heart. As to what we want – it's to help you in your research into the murder of poor Mr. Potter. That's all."

"How do you intend to do that? I'll follow this story wherever it leads. Nobody tells me what to write."

Williams's smile vanished. He slid a large manila envelope across the table to her.

"Spare me the indignation, Emma. Here's a list of people you should talk to. You've made a pretty good start on identifying individuals who might have wanted Potter dead, but there is a lot more to learn. These people can fill in a lot of the gaps in your research. Think of me as your research assistant, providing leads for you to follow up. My team has been doing some preliminary background work for you."

"Who's this team of yours?"

"We're not part of your story Emma. It would be a mistake to write about us - a serious mistake. But to satisfy your curiosity – see the man sitting at the bar over there – the big guy with the military haircut and the baseball hat. He's on the team. And the small Japanese woman with the yellow shirt who's just coming out of the restaurant – she's on the team too."

Emma watched as Williams looked to the woman in the yellow shirt and raised his head slightly, and her response – a clear shake of the head from side to side before she turned and went back into the restaurant. Williams smiled another one of his cold smiles.

"I'm impressed Emma. It's smart of you to keep all your notes and such on a memory device you carry with you or encrypted somewhere in the cloud. It would be far too easy for someone to find your research on your laptop or in your room. And make no mistake, Emma, there are serious people involved here."

Emma had lost her appetite and said little as she listened to Williams outline for her in some detail various aspects of Potter's background that warranted further looking into, as well as the multiple benefits that the Lily Bay development would bring to the Moosehead Lake region.

When their waitress cleared the dishes and Williams covered the check with two twenties and placed his hands on the table to rise, he leaned forward and spoke in a low voice.

"This is your big chance Emma. Play your cards right and there could be a substantial bonus for you when this is all over – maybe a permanent job and a steady paycheck will be waiting. Just don't fuck it up."

Emma stayed sitting at the table for several minutes after Williams left, trying to stop her hands from shaking. When she got back up to her room her suspicions were confirmed. Someone – probably the woman in the yellow shirt - had searched her room and managed to breach her security settings and access her computer files. Fortunately all her notes and the recordings of her interviews were on the flash drive nestled in her pocket.

12.
COWBOY
MONDAY

Cowboy had fixated on Anne over the weekend, compiling a massive collection of articles and images of her from the internet and using his 600mm telephoto lens to photograph her on the dock of her camp on the south shore of Sebec Lake. Trailing her to Shaw's Supermarket on Sunday he picked up a few things for dinner and watched from another checkout line as Anne chatted with the cashier and bag girl, both of whom clearly knew her. It looked like she might be an accomplished cook, judging from the items she bought, and Cowboy fantasized about what she would cook for him once they were married.

When Anne headed into work on Monday Cowboy was waiting and pulled in behind her, always keeping several cars between them. He was surprised when Anne turned left on the Milo Road at the post office in Dover-Foxcroft instead of continuing on to the sheriff's office and courthouse. His excitement slowly mounted as she drove into Milo and turned right up the hill by Elaine's Café onto Pleasant Street. When Anne turned right again onto Willow Street, Cowboy was ecstatic – she was headed for Becky Crawford's house.

He drove past Willow, turned around and parked at the intersection of Pleasant and Willow. He wasn't sure if the microphones he had hidden in Becky's house would transmit this far, but it was worth a try. Ignoring the stares of several kids pedaling by on their bikes, he smiled to himself as he picked up Becky and Anne's conversation loud and clear through his earbuds.

Becky seemed barely coherent - whimpering and answering

Anne's questions with brief whispered responses. A third woman, probably Heather back from her romantic weekend on the coast, was trying to calm Becky down and comfort her. Becky kept saying it wasn't her fault and that her father wouldn't understand – blurting out that her assailant had a big knife, and he tied her up. Shuddering as she described the tape recording of the wedding ceremony and the vows, Becky had no memory of what happened after he gave her the pill. Anne hoped she really had been unconscious during the rape rather than repressing her memory of the assault. Becky was able, with Heather's encouragement, to talk about her young Christian discussion group at the Charleston Church and her online interaction with the Christian community. She said she did not use Christian dating sites and could not think of anyone in particular who showed an interest in her through her church or online activities. This line of questioning concerned Cowboy and he furtively glanced at passing traffic. Anne appeared to be working from a profile that was being developed and he wondered if the police might have begun to monitor some of his target groups. Cowboy's concern intensified as Anne began to include Heather in her questioning and began asking the two housemates about anyone following them or any recent unusual encounters. Heather turned out to have much more useful information than Becky.

She remembered noticing a strange man at Elaine's Bakery and Café a week or so ago. They had been seated at a table by the window when he came in. He had briefly glanced in their direction before walking over to the counter and ordering several donuts and coffee, which he then took back out onto the side porch. He was still there, sitting at a table on the porch when they left a half hour or so later. They walked right by him on the way to their car. He had eaten the donuts and finished his coffee but was still just sitting there, gazing blankly at the river running through town. Heather said she could feel his eyes on their back as they walked toward the parking lot, and it creeped her out.

Anne asked Heather what she could remember about the man at

Elaine's, and Cowboy held his breath as he listened to her response. She described a medium sized individual, well-muscled, with black, shoulder length, greasy hair and a slight limp – he seemed to drag his right foot a bit. He was clean-shaven and wore a baseball hat pushed back on his head – it might have been a Boston Red Sox hat. His new-looking jeans were held up with a belt having a large oval buckle – like a rodeo prize buckle, and his well-worn blue denim shirt was western cut and had pearl snaps instead of buttons.

Anne then asked if either of them had noticed a white pickup following them or parked on their street, and Cowboy sat frozen behind the wheel as Heather provided a detailed description of his truck – an older model white Ford Ranger, just like the one her father had when she was growing up, that had been parked right next to their car in the parking lot at Elaine's. It had a small crack in the windshield, a dent in the right rear fender, and several empty plastic bottles – Coke maybe, in the bed of the pickup.

Cowboy checked the rearview mirror and pulled slowly out onto Pleasant Street, planning a back way up to his place that would hopefully avoid any surveillance Anne might attempt on the main roads. Reaching in the glove box he extracted a 9mm Glock automatic and placed it on the passenger seat, covering it with his hat. He was already planning a visit to Anne's cabin as soon as he could arrange it – she was begging to be brought under his guidance and control. He went north out of Milo, turned west on a little traveled back road, and then drove south through Sebec Village down to Atkinson, where he turned west, coming into Dover-Foxcroft the back way past Brown's Mill.

Making it safely through downtown, he was just past the Wild Monkey Hair Salon when he saw the flashing blue lights behind him. Pulling over, Cowboy watched the sheriff's deputy step out of his patrol car, put his hat on, and approach the truck with a relaxed stride. The deputy looked like a teenager, tall and gangly – it would be a shame to have to kill him, Cowboy thought to himself. Frowning when he noticed a body camera attached to the deputy's protective vest, he moved the Glock into the crotch of his pants, fingering off the safety. He could not allow his face to be photographed, and shifting in his seat so he could shoot the deputy in the head before he reached the driver's side door of the truck, Cowboy started to raise the gun from his lap.

The deputy had stopped his approach to the truck, turning to listen to the squawk of his radio in the Crown Vic cruiser. Pausing briefly before turning back to return to his car, the deputy called a quick explanation to Cowboy:

"Just a friendly heads up sir. Your left rear tail light is out – please get it repaired as soon as you get a chance."

Smiling at the deputy's good fortune, Cowboy re-engaged the safety on his handgun, placed it back on the passenger seat, and waited until the deputy turned around and headed back into town before pulling out.

The rest of the trip home was uneventful and Cowboy pulled the truck into a back corner of the barn behind a stack of moldy hay bales. Moving over into another alcove he pulled a tarp off of a rusted 1996 Honda Accord that at some point in its past life had been painted primer black, apparently with a brush. Hand painted under the driver's side window in yellow capital letters was the name the car had been given; certainly tongue in cheek – "Chick Magnet." Cowboy wasn't surprised when the car wouldn't start– he would have to switch over the battery from the truck. The Chick Magnet had been in the barn when he first rented the property and his landlord had gladly sold it to him, as is, for a few hundred dollars. The Honda would have to do for the few weeks remaining until he pulled up stakes and torched the barn and the two vehicles he would leave behind. Grabbing a wire brush off the workbench, he removed the name "Chick Magnet" from the driver's door – no need to draw any attention to the car or jog anyone's memory of the Honda's previous life. Returning to his RV, Cowboy pulled his suitcase out from under the bed and started to assemble his wedding night kit for his visit that evening to Anne's south shore cabin. He laid all the items he would take with him out on the counter, placed them in the order he would need them, and then went through his usual visual sequencing exercise to make sure he wasn't forgetting anything. He replaced the batteries in both his flashlight and small recorder, and then slipped everything into his backpack.

Moving over to the closet Cowboy took off his western style snap shirt and exchanged it for a Carhartt shirt he had recently bought at the Indian Hill Trading Post in Greenville. Stripping his belt off, he removed the oval rodeo belt buckle, threw it in the trash, and selected a simple nondescript replacement belt from his closet. His next stop was the bathroom, where he cut his hair quite short and used one of the hair dyes he kept on hand to turn his hair strawberry blond. Pleased with his transformation, he returned to the Chick Magnet, replaced its battery, and drove it up to Greenville for a wash and a fill-up and to make sure all the lights were working – he certainly did not want to be pulled over later that night.

Cowboy made his usual pre-matrimony dinner that night – chicken fried steak and beans – what he usually had eaten back at the Waldo Compound. He took a shower, shaved, and brushed his teeth, then sat down to watch a movie before heading out to Anne's cabin. He was a big Doris Day fan, and selected "Pillow Talk" for his evening's entertainment, even though he had watched it so often he knew most of the dialogue by heart. The movie ended about eleven and Cowboy headed down to Anne's place on Sebec Lake in the Chick Magnet. Rather than drive anywhere close to where Anne lived, Cowboy drove up around to the north shore of Sebec Lake, parked at the Newell Cove public boat ramp, and then "borrowed" a kayak from a nearby camp and paddled across the lake to Anne's camp.

It was a cloudless night with a good breeze out of the west, and the sound of the waves on the rocks lining the lakeshore had masked Cowboy's approach to Anne's cabin. Sitting up against the partially restored boathouse, he watched the fireflies in the tall grass bordering the lake, and occasionally checked his watch. He figured three AM would be about right for the commencement of the marriage ceremony. The Big Dipper was bright in the night sky and he thought back to the many evenings he had spent on the roof of the dormitory building in Waldo, New Mexico, gazing at the heavens and avoiding the quick fists of the Patriarch.

Cowboy was not optimistic about Anne agreeing to marry him and give birth to their child, and was puzzling over what he should do. He figured he probably would ask her what she wanted – to die right there in her home or promise to bear their son or daughter. It was probably better if he killed her either way, he concluded–her poking into his business was beginning to get on his nerves.

Pulling on his latex gloves Cowboy moved quietly to the side door of Anne's cabin and was surprised to find the screen door unlatched. Crossing the porch he crouched in front of the door that led from the screen porch to the kitchen and set his backpack on the floor. The door's Yale lock looked to be an old one and didn't present much of a challenge. Opening up the tool roll that held his lock pick set, he took out a tension wrench and raking pick and set to work. After six rakes, the lock's driver pins had all been pushed up and secured above the sheer line, and the kitchen door swung open with an audible squeak. Cowboy froze in place for several minutes, listening for any sounds that might indicate that Anne had heard the squeak of the door opening. Confident that his entry had gone unnoticed, he stepped over to the kitchen table and set his backpack down. Seeing movement out of the corner of his eye, he turned his head and was momentarily disconcerted to see a large white cat watching him from the kitchen counter. They gazed at each other for a while across the dark kitchen and then Anne's cat Charley jumped down from the counter and padded silently out of the room.

Carefully unzipping his pack, Cowboy began to select the items he would need first to secure Anne and began humming contentedly to himself – he could come back to the kitchen for his pack once she was restrained. He had just placed his Bowie knife, blindfold, zip ties, and flashlight on the table when he thought he heard a slight sound from the direction of Anne's bedroom. Picking up the knife and flashlight, he took a few steps toward the corridor leading off the kitchen when he heard another sound – one that he knew well from his time in the military – the distinctive 'snick' of a round being chambered in an automatic weapon.

Turning quickly, Cowboy grabbed his pack off the kitchen table, bumping into the table and knocking the zip ties and blindfold to the floor. Running full tilt out the open door to the screen porch and slamming through the screen door, he vaulted off the steps and sprinted toward the cover and relative safety of the boathouse. Cowboy had just rounded the corner, out of sight, when a bright light began sweeping the forest edge from the screen porch doorway, and he could hear Anne's strong, confident voice call out to him.

"Don't be in such a hurry, Cowboy, let's sit down and have a little chat about putting the baby." Her taunting voice followed him as he moved further into the woods, along the shoreline, keeping the boathouse between him and Anne's cabin. Anne was eager to follow Cowboy but wasn't sure whether he was armed and was hesitant about venturing into the woods wearing only a T-shirt.

Anne went back into the cabin and called the sheriff's office, and within twenty minutes city police and sheriff's cars had arrived and began searching the few roads that led into her neighborhood. With the exception of a teenage couple parked at the end of a little used dead-end gravel road, they turned up nothing. No white pickup, no Cowboy. He seemed to have had vanished into thin air.

Carefully picking his way east about a hundred yards along the rocky shoreline of Sebec Lake, Cowboy located the kayak he had stolen on the north shore earlier that night and began his journey back across the lake. He struggled to stay on course, with a freshening breeze from the west pushing waves against the side of the kayak. Despite his best efforts to avoid the dangerous shallows and rocks just west of Pine Island, he struck a submerged boulder and capsized. Holding onto the paddle and struggling to gain a footing, he watched the kayak slip away from him in the darkness. It took him only ten minutes or so to crawl through the rocky shallows and reach the west side of Pine Island and then walk over to the rental cabin on the opposite shore. Finding a flashlight in the unoccupied cabin, Cowboy looked for a rowboat or canoe he could use to reach his car on the north shore, which he had left at the Newell Cove public boat ramp. The only watercraft on the island, it turned out, was a small white two-seat paddleboat, and the disturbed killer made quite a strange tableau as he slowly paddled a vessel usually powered by vacationing children across to the boat ramp where he had left his car. Wet and angry, Cowboy headed home in the Chick Magnet, already thinking about the different ways he might employ to kill Anne Quinn.

It was a good forty-minute drive from Doug's home on the north shore around the eastern end of Sebec Lake to Anne's cabin, but by boat he was only five minutes away. Anne heard the growl of his vintage Chris Craft inboard – a 1952 Sportsman, soon after she called to tell him about the visit from the Cowboy. Putting on her ratty plaid bathrobe she walked out to her dock with a light to guide him in.

After a brief embrace, and Anne's assurances that she was unharmed, she led him back into her kitchen and pointed out the blindfold and zip ties on the floor.

"I had gotten up to check on Charlie's food dish – he woke me up with his head butting, and that usually means I forgot to fill it. But halfway to the bedroom door I heard someone in the kitchen, humming to himself. The freak was in my kitchen, humming a happy tune."

Doug led Anne over to the leather couch in her living room before going back to the kitchen and reaching up on the shelf next to the refrigerator for the Jack Daniels. Pouring them each a healthy tumbler, he sat next to her on the couch as she continued.

"He must have heard me chambering a round and took off like a bat outta hell. By the time I had grabbed a flashlight and got to the door he was already in the woods – no idea where he went, but cars are out looking for him, and there aren't too many roads out of here."

"Did you hear a car?"

"No – nothing. And I've been watching for a white pickup truck – that's what we think he's driving."

"It didn't take him long to target you Anne – he must be watching his victims, seen you interviewing them, and has now focused on you as a result."

Anne took another healthy slug from her glass of Jack Daniels and leaned back, closing her eyes and taking a long deep breath.

"What now Doug. What should I do?"

"Tonight, we'll stay here, if you have a spare toothbrush, and tomorrow we'll figure something out. Maybe you should stay at my place on the north shore until we catch this freak – I have a pretty good security system, and we can see how good you are at Scrabble."

13
DOUGLAS
TUESDAY

Spencer's Bakery and Cafe was crowded when Anne and Doug came through the front door at about 9:30 on Tuesday morning. They had stayed up talking and drinking Jack Daniels after the Cowboy had been run off the night before, and both were hung over. Kate Bishop showed them to a booth that had just been vacated and asked if Anne was OK. Anne realized that word of the Cowboy's break-in had spread quickly, and scanning the room noticed June Torben sitting with several friends and gazing at her over the top of her coffee cup. Anne and Doug ordered quickly – both opted for the biggest breakfast on the menu – the Lumberjack Special, and settled back with coffee as June walked over to the booth and slid in next to Anne. The cafe got noticeably quieter.

"What happened last night Anne? Are you OK?"

"I'm good. Some guy broke into the cabin in the middle of the night, but Charley head-butted me awake in time and I was able to run him off. I called Doug and he offered to stay over in case the guy thought about coming back."

June waited for Anne to say more, but she just smiled demurely and Doug concentrated on twirling his coffee cup on the table and gazing over toward the pastry display. June realized neither Anne nor Doug were going to say more about last night, and she ended up doing most of the talking as Anne and Doug worked through their Lumberjack Specials – a two-egg cheese and red pepper omelet, hash browns, a rasher of bacon, and biscuits on the side. June complained at length about what a jerk Sheriff Hudson was and how he was driving her husband Jim to distraction. Hoping – unsuccessfully, to elicit some sort of response from Anne, June realized that Doug and Anne were not really listening to her, just nodding at appropriate points and stealing glances across the table at each other.

Doug's phone vibrated in his pocket. Answering, he walked over to the front door, spoke briefly, and returning to the booth, leaned in and kissed Anne.

"That was Chief Marcus – they found the other axe in the water off Sugar Island. I'm heading up to Greenville. I'll call you in a little while."

The axe was laid out on a table in the Greenville police station, along with Rick Potter's watch fob, which was missing several of its attachments. Chief Marcus doubted the discovery would help the investigation much.

"They found the axe on the bottom twenty yards or so straight out from the dock, with the charm bracelet thing wrapped around it. I doubt we'll get any DNA or prints but I'll send it down to Augusta to give it a try."

"Nothing much new from my end on either killing," Doug responded. "Tom Richard called and updated me on the way up here – he's checked all the court records for any recent or ongoing cases involving either Potter or Breen, and nothing jumped out. Do you have anyone worth following up on here?"

"Not really," Marcus answered. "We've talked to a lot of people who knew the victims – relatives, friends, and business associates, as well as individuals they have had run-ins with, and didn't turn anything up. We also haven't picked up anything from our sources. We got nothin'."

Marcus paused, checked his watch, and continued.

"There is one person we could talk to, though – Paul Minnis. He lives out in the middle of nowhere – literally. We'll have to take a floatplane up north to his lake. Chip Wills, a local pilot, is waiting for my call and is ready to take us up there this morning if you're up for it. Chip's doing one of his regular supply runs up to the remote lakes west of the Allagash and he'll drop us off and pick us up on his way back. We should be back by mid-afternoon. I talked with Minnis and after checking you out he's willing to give us a few hours of his time. He's kind of an odd character, a brainiac, and definitely paranoid. He said he would do a little research on Potter and Breen and see what he can come up with. He might find something for us, or it could be a bust."

Chief Marcus paused before continuing, seeming to decide what else to say.

"I've known Paul since the second grade. He was always into computers, as soon as they came on the scene, and he got a scholarship to MIT after graduation from Foxcroft Academy. I'm not sure he ever finished college – he got hired by the Feds and worked in some hush-hush program for a while before going freelance. Now he works as a consultant I guess, assessing computer security for federal agencies and private companies. He doesn't talk about it, just jokingly refers to himself as a 'hacker for hire.' As they drove the short distance over to the West Cove, Doug texted Anne to let her know he would be out of cell phone contact until late in the afternoon, and added "7PM – your place or mine?"

A light wind out of the north riffled the water as Wills' vintage 1954 deHavilland Beaver lifted off from West Cove at Greenville. Along with Bateman and Marcus it carried several hundred pounds of deliveries for the fishing camps and resorts Wills regularly supplied on a half dozen remote northern lakes. Doug had flown over the vast northern forests of Maine a number of other times and he never ceased to marvel at the seemingly endless expanse of green stretching toward the horizon. Moosehead Lake was a dark, cold blue beneath them as they flew north past Sugar Island, over the gray 800-foot rhyolite cliffs of Mt. Kineo, and across the lake's Northwest Cove. Angling northwest at Seeboomook, on the north shore of Northwest Cove, the former location of a WWII prisoner of war camp, they flew another half hour across an unbroken expanse of forest, crossing the Allagash River, before Wills decreased altitude, circled, and made a smooth landing along the long axis of a lake that looked devoid of any human habitation. Wills only smiled in response when Doug asked if they had landed on the right lake.

They had motored within about 200 yards of the east end of the lake when Doug noticed a small battered outboard moving toward them from shore, piloted by a large man with a beard. Chip killed the plane's engine, stepped down on one of the pontoons, and opening one of the plane's large rear doors, started sorting through a pile of packages. Marcus grabbed the mooring line that the bearded man in the boat tossed to him, made it fast, and climbed into the boat. Doug followed, and after introducing himself to Paul Minnis, the bearded man, he took the packages Chip handed down to him and stowed them between the boat's seats. With a wave and a "thanks" to Wills, Minnis, who looked scruffy in a ragged flannel shirt and faded jeans, turned the boat in a smooth curve and headed back to land.

Doug couldn't see a dock or any evidence of a house as they approached the heavily wooded shoreline. The trees were massive, and taller than any Doug had ever seen before in northern Maine. He looked at Minnis with a questioning expression, and Minnis smiled as he responded to Doug's obvious question.

"You've landed in a rare surviving patch of ancient forest. It's never seen a lumberjack or an axe. The Eagle Lake old growth preserves east of here are much better known, and have been popularized, but there are other remaining old growth stands that still survive. This is the largest, but only a few people know about it and even fewer have seen it. It's the reason I bought the lake and the surrounding forest."

Minnis killed the engine as the boat slid up onto a small sandy beach. Doug and Chief Marcus climbed out and were passed an armful of packages to carry as they were led up a narrow path. Doug glanced up from the trail, and looking into the forest, was surprised to notice a single story flat-roofed house set in among the trees just twenty yards or so in front of them. The entire front of the house was large glass panels and sliding doors that reflected the surrounding forest, making the structure almost invisible from the nearby lakeshore. High above, the overstory canopy extended unbroken above the house. Glancing around, Doug set his load of packages down on the ground-level deck that extended along the front of the house and asked an obvious question.

"Where do you get your power?"

"Mostly it's from a series of river turbines set in two nearby streams that feed into the lake. I have a backup gas generator but so far I've never needed it. But even I'm not crazy enough to live here in the winter. I stay from just after ice-out in the spring till just before the lake ices over in the fall."

Sliding open one of the massive glass doors, Minnis led Bateman and Marcus into a large open floor plan room. The view out the window wall was stunning – framed by massive old growth pines, the lake sparkled in the mid-day sun, and a pair of loons could be seen in the near distance. The floor and walls of the room were aged pine. A kitchen alcove held a small four-burner stove, pine cabinets, soapstone countertops and sink, and a large espresso machine. Along the back wall a half-open door showed a glass-walled hallway leading to a separate structure, probably a bedroom suite. Motioning his guests to a large brown leather couch with a great view west down the lake, Minnis asked if they wanted coffee. Bateman and Marcus both nodded, and Minnis brewed three large cups before sitting across from them in a matching leather club chair. Behind him, at the far end of the room, a U-shaped desk had several dozen fountain pens scattered across it and held three large computer screens, all of which were dark.

Leaning back in his chair, Minnis gazed out at the lake, looked at Doug, and began.

"The chief has vouched for you Detective Bateman – he says you can be trusted. You appear to be a straight shooter, and Signorina Elettra didn't turn up anything concerning about you. So with a few ground rules, I can try to help with your investigation."

Seeing Doug's puzzled expression, Minnis looked amused and explained.

"Elettra is what I call my computer system - it's named for the computer sleuth secretary in Donna Leon's Commissario Guido Brunetti mysteries. I'm a big fan of Leon's books and Signorina Elettra's ability to access information on the Internet, even when it is protected by supposedly unbreachable security. That's basically what I enjoy doing. So if you're willing to agree to a few things, I can try to be of some help in the investigation."

"What are the ground rules?" Doug asked.

"Well, can you both confirm that you do not have any recording devices?"

Doug and Chief Marcus both nodded.

"I'll print out the main bullet points for you of what I have learned, which unfortunately is not much. It's for your eyes only, and while it might help you to identify worthwhile lines of inquiry, none of it can be used in any prosecution – you'll need to find independent corroborating evidence. And of course, I'll insist on a clear commitment on your part of what we could call 'use immunity.' That simply means I will deny being the source of any of this information and any perceived illegalities that might be associated with how I obtained it."

Doug responded.

"That all sounds good to me."

"OK," Minnis replied. "And keep in mind, I have an excellent working relationship with national intelligence entities and law enforcement, so even if you decided to make problems for me, it wouldn't go well for you."

Doug smiled.

"How good is your on the ground security here, Mr. Minnis?"

"You don't want to test it Doug. And your ex-Seal colleague Tom Richard's Ghillie suit and bag of tricks wouldn't do him much good either. I have a quite good system, installed by friends who owe me a few favors. And it's not a passive security system – it bites."

"Richard A. Potter," Minnis continued, not waiting for a response. "Sorry to say, no clear potential killers for little Rick really jumped out at me. He was a pretty sad character, all in all. He had a complicated, warped, family background. His grandfather Albert Gremill, rejected by the military during WWII - moral turpitude apparently, worked odd jobs, and for the government during WWII over at Seeboomook, and then turned to crime after the war. He went to prison for a lengthy term in the early fifties and Rick's grandmother got a divorce and raised his dad Percy on her own. She died when Percy was only seven or so, and a very wealthy elderly couple – the Potters, adopted Percy. Percy inherited all of the Potter's companies and properties when they passed away, and promptly married a beauty queen from South Carolina. Rick was their only child and was raised mostly by nannies before being sent off to boarding school at a young age. He really didn't get to know his adoptive parents much before they died in an avalanche vacationing in the Swiss Alps."

Minnis paused, took a sip of his coffee, and continued.

"Little Rick never married – too fascinated with himself I guess. He was never part of the community here and most people found him to be a self-important bore. He was all puffed up and always focused on constructing an alternate reality in which he cast himself as a mover and shaker, a pillar of the community, and the scion of a very prominent, well-respected family dynasty. I don't think there are any irate husbands out there – Potter didn't hit on married women – he mostly tried to impress a string of younger women who hadn't yet been subjected to his long boring efforts at self-promotion. The women he dated never stuck around for very long."

Minnis took another sip of coffee and picked up the narrative.

"Judging from his various bank and brokerage records it's clear that at the same time that he was spinning his little alternative reality for himself and showing his watch fob to anyone willing to listen, Rick was also making lots of bad business deals and throwing away the family fortune at an impressive rate. His exclusive high-end fishing and hunting camps were not doing well and he ended up having to sell off most of his timber holdings to cover his bad deals. Then came liquidation of his stake in a number of local businesses, and in the last year or so his email accounts show that he had been doing a lot of online betting, with disastrous results."

Raising his hand, Doug interrupted.

"So who do you think had a motive to kill him?"

"Well, I ranked the top five for you in my written dossier. In fifth place is the contractor who got stiffed on tens of thousands of dollars of renovations on the Potter compound on Sugar Island. Fourth is the business partners on the local airport development who haven't been paid what Potter owed them. Third place I would give to local timber-cutting outfits who according to court records are suing him for short-changing them on profits from harvesting from his properties – these are hard men who are not used to being crossed. Second place goes to the development syndicate planning the Lily Bay golf course communities – Little Rick appeared to have really pissed them off for no apparent reason. My top candidate for axing him is the Boston faction of the Patriarca crime family – the New England Mafia. Little Rick was in to them for several hundred thousand dollars from his sports betting when he was killed, and he was ignoring their requests for payment. It doesn't make much sense for them to knock off someone who owes them money, I realize, but their internal communications suggest they might have been prepared to write off the losses and make an example of him. I would have expected some sort of calling card, however – maybe a betting slip stuffed in his mouth."

Minnis paused and Doug responded.

"These are all good leads Paul. We really appreciate your help. What can you tell us about Virginia Breen?"

"Breen is pretty much the opposite of Little Rick. He went from riches to rags; she grew up poor and turned her small real estate company into a large multinational property acquisition and investment empire. The oldest of six kids, Virginia worked in the potato fields of Aroostook County and as a waitress in high school, got a partial scholarship and continued waitressing during her undergrad years at the University of Maine, majoring in business. She got into real estate after college, starting as a sales agent, but showed an early talent for spotting properties with up-market potential. She formed her own company eventually, brought her brother into the business, and started attracting major investors. Breen steadily built the business, went international, but never forgot her northern Maine roots."

Minnis paused, sipped his coffee, and continued.

"Her bank records, tax filings, and financial transactions are complicated, as you might imagine, but they looked mostly kosher up till about five years ago – then I started noticing big wire transfers into her realty acquisition accounts from overseas banks – mostly in Cyprus. I'm still working on tracing those funds back further, but would guess that they were funneled through shell companies and will be hard to track. At about the same time, her company began acquiring a variety of land parcels, large and small, scattered seemingly randomly across the middle of Maine. There may be a motive hidden somewhere in there, but so far I haven't been able to see it."

Minnis paused and Doug asked.

"So nothing promising turned up?"

"Other than the recent flurry of land acquisitions funded by unknown overseas actors, I admit, I came up empty. Her brother Gary, of course, should be on your short list – they had a serious falling out about the time the Cyprus cash inflow began. She cut him right out of the company then, and he is one angry sibling. It got nasty. So he certainly has a personal motive for wishing her harm and might also be able to shed light on her business dealings back then."

Minnis stood, indicating that the discussion was over, and offered to show them around his place in the time left before Chip returned.

As Chip Wills landed the deHavilland Beaver back in Greenville,

Doug checked his phone and listened to a voice mail from Anne.

"My place, whenever you can get here. Sauvignon blanc is chilling. Pick up some of the large lump crabmeat at Graves there in Greenville. Call me."

14
ANNE
WEDNESDAY

It was a little after eight in the morning. Anne lay in bed with Charlie curled up purring on the pillow next to her. The sun was streaming in the bedroom window and she could hear the laughter of several kayakers paddling past her camp on the south shore of Sebec Lake. Doug had left a half hour or so ago, needing to drive back to his place for a change of clothes before heading up to Greenville to follow up on several of the leads Minnis had come up with.

Last evening had been good. Wearing a sleeveless white blouse that she had had for ages, along with a worn pair of shorts and flip-flops, Anne had greeted Doug with a kiss and a chilled glass of wine as he walked in the kitchen door with a plastic container of crabmeat. Taking the container, she admired the large chunks of fresh crab as she poured it into a mixing bowl on the kitchen island and began putting the crab cakes together – combining the crabmeat with finely diced red, yellow and orange bell pepper, along with a poblano for a little heat. Anne added some basil and green onion, a raw egg, a shot of Worcestershire and Tobasco, and just enough mayonnaise to hold the crab and peppers together. Forming the mixture into patties she coated them with panko breadcrumbs and slid them into a cast iron pan with olive oil and butter. The pan went on top of the six-burner industrial stove she had found for sale the year before in a closed restaurant down in Dexter. The roast corn salad, still warm from the oven, was already on the table – kernels from four fresh cobs that she had picked up from Stutzman's Farm Stand that afternoon, combined with diced red onion and black beans and roasted for half an hour, then tossed with lime, cilantro and green onion.

Doug sat at the small wooden kitchen table – simple yellow placemats, thrift shop knives and forks, paper napkins, two candles, and the corn salad. As she made the crab cakes and slid them into the pan to cook – just three minutes on a side, Anne talked about her day and her lack of progress on the Cowboy rapes. She had not as yet found any connections between the two victims – they didn't know each other, had no friends or acquaintances in common, had different cable providers, different propane providers, shopped at different markets, and did not frequent the same bars or restaurants.

Doug was listening quietly, occasionally taking a sip of his wine, and watching her with a relaxed intensity that made her turn from the stove and ask.

"What are you looking at? What's going on?"

Doug smiled.

"I'm looking at a beautiful woman cooking me dinner and telling me about her day. I'm watching the sunlight on your hair, noticing your long legs, the cat on the counter picking up a stray piece of crab, and feeling the sweet breeze off the lake. I feel happy Anne, for the first time in a long time. It feels like school just got out and the whole summer is stretching out in front of us. Like vacation just started. Can life be this simple? This easy?"

Anne took three short steps over to where Doug was sitting, straddled him and sat on his lap. Smiling, pressing up against him, she leaned in, and he could feel her breasts against his chest and her breath on his ear as she answered his question in a whisper.

"Yes, Douglas, I think so."

As Doug began to embrace her, Anne jumped up and moved quickly back to the stove and the crab cakes, adding over her shoulder.

"But first we need to find out what you think about my cooking."

After dinner they sat out on the dock and let the evening unfold.

A family line of mergansers swam by – a mother followed by six young of the year. A kingfisher chittered as it flew along the shore. A patio boat pulled shrieking kids on tubes in circles over by Pine Island, where two baby eagles perched on the edge of their nest, flapping their wings in anticipation of their first flight.

The temperature dropped as the sun disappeared below the tree line, and reaching over, Anne took Doug's hand and led him back to the cabin.

Checking the clock on her bedside table, Anne forced herself to get up, showered, had a quick breakfast, and headed into work. She had been watching for a white Ford Ranger pickup truck ever since Becky's roommate Heather had described it the day before yesterday, and her Glock sidearm was within easy reach on the passenger seat next to her. But she took no notice of the beat-up black Honda Accord – the Chick Magnet, when it pulled out of the Dunkin Donuts just west of town and followed her. It drove on past down Main Street when she pulled in and parked at the sheriff's office, but then turned around in the Bangor Savings Bank parking lot and parked across the street. Cowboy watched Anne enter the building before getting out of the Chick Magnet, crossing the street, and going into the Rite Aid Pharmacy located next to the sheriff's office. He came out a few minutes later with one of their five-dollar Dover-Foxcroft T-shirts, a large diet coke, and a bag of pretzels. Ready for a long wait if need be, he settled back behind the wheel of the Chick Magnet. He figured he would follow Anne at a discreet distance until he saw an opening, and then finish her. As he thought about how it could unfold, Cowboy reached down to the sheath on his belt by his right hip and touched the handle of his Ka-Bar D2 Extreme combat knife. He had carried it throughout his military service and always kept it close at hand. This was not the big shiny knife he used to impress his fiancés – this was his killing knife. And he was good with it.

As soon as she sat down at her desk Anne checked her emails and saw a message to call Patty Crown at Quantico. Picking up her phone, she called the number Patty had given her. The FBI agent answered on the second ring.

"Thanks for calling me Anne. I'm glad I caught you. I have a lot of information on this guy we decided to call the Cowboy. I'll send you my report by email in a few days, once it's complete, but I wanted to give you a heads-up before that."

Noting the unconcealed anxiety in Patty's voice, Anne voiced a brief "thanks Patty," and asked what she had found.

"Cowboy didn't show up in the ViCAP database – not too surprising I guess, but when I started querying state and regional databases and followed up with emails and phone calls to law enforcement units that had made promising entries, the Cowboy showed up all over the place. We have the beginning of a geographical pattern that's pretty distinct but doesn't seem to make a lot of sense."

"What kind of a pattern?"

"That's what's so weird. If these are all Cowboy incidents, they pop up as isolated clusters of rapes – three or four, five at most, in each cluster, assuming we have all of the rapes, and we may not. The first loose cluster is in south Texas, spread along the borderlands. Four rapes, the whole marriage ceremony thing, with brides marked by ear notching – a triangle cut out of their right ears. These look like the start for the Cowboy – pretty poorly planned – one in broad daylight with Cowboy wearing a mask – no large knife to scare the victims, no Ketamine, and more of a pleading, insecure narrative."

Patty Crown paused, and Anne could hear rustling paper in the background.

"Let's see… the next cluster is in southern Illinois – Carbondale, Cape Girardeau, Murphysboro, the following year. Three rapes, this time all at night and the victims carefully selected – he's refining his attack strategy – still cropping ears. Then, just six months later, in the Park City area east of Salt Lake City, three rapes in a period of five weeks, and now he has started to brand, but the brands are not numbers, it looks like a cattle brand – a stylized 'WCF.' Then there's a gap of several years – we probably are missing one or more clusters, and he pops up suddenly in Virginia – down around Williamsburg – two William and Mary coeds raped and branded with the 'WCF' in just a week, and by now he's using Ketamine and a big knife."

Patty Crown paused again, probably consulting her notes.

"Then, about three years ago, he drops off the radar completely, until now. Judging from the numbers '9' and '10' on your victims, there are two or three other clusters in the last several years that we haven't yet picked up, the ones including the brands '1' through '8.' I'm still trying to identify the likely missing clusters but it won't be that easy, given the seeming random nature of his movements around the country and the way he abruptly appears and disappears."

With a growing sense of dread, Anne interrupted Patty's narrative.

"Patty, Cowboy broke into my home Monday night. Fortunately I woke up, but he ran before I got a shot at him. Looks like I may have attracted his interest."

"Jesus Anne, you need protection, and you may not have much time to catch the Cowboy before he moves on. It's not clear what determines how long he stays in an area, or how he selects his victims. But what is clear is that he doesn't stick around long – a month or so in any one locale. Do you have any leads?"

"We've got nothing Patty. Not a thing. He probably drives, or drove, a white Ford Ranger pickup, but we have no recent sightings, so he might have ditched it or left town already. We also have a vague description – average white male, maybe in his 30s, long greasy hair, rodeo belt buckle, cowboy snap shirt, maybe a gimpy leg. That's it."

"Send me what you have Anne – to me directly, not to the ViCap, and also any DNA you've recovered – both from the rapes and your break-in. I've asked investigators who worked the other clusters to also send DNA and prints. We should be able to get solid forensic links between the clusters."

"I'll get our lab to get the DNA samples down to you as quick as we can. We didn't recover any prints – which is surprising. He isn't reluctant about DNA – of course he wants to impregnate his victims, but why then be so careful about prints?"

"He must be pretty confident we don't have his DNA on file," Patty replied. "But must also know that his prints are in records somewhere – a run-in with the law or military records, probably."

"Another avenue we can take on the DNA," Patty added, "is to work the publicly accessible DNA databases like Ancestry.com – maybe we can identify a relative of Cowboy and work toward identifying him that way. And I'll also drill down on the first cluster along the border– looking both for any likely candidates who have a record of rape or other crimes against women, and any clues about what 'WCF' might stand for. The belt buckle and snap shirt fits with the branding – maybe he's from Texas."

Patty said that she would send the files on the earlier clusters to Anne as email attachments, and then asked directly.

"Anne, you are going to get round the clock protection, right?"

"Well, I doubt the sheriff will go for that, but I just acquired a live-in state police detective, so my evenings are covered. I'll see if I can get someone assigned to partner up with me during work hours until this is over."

"Make sure it happens Anne. This Cowboy character has gotten very good at what he does – he's a seasoned predator – careful, methodical, and very dangerous."

Cowboy decided he didn't like the parking place on Main Street. People walking by and passing in cars could get too good a look at him and the Chick Magnet. So he moved over to the Rite Aid Pharmacy parking lot, picking a spot way in the back next to an area of dense bushes and out of range of the security cameras. Angling his side mirror and rear view mirror, he had good sight lines to the entrance to the sheriff's office and Anne's Toyota Land Cruiser and was partially shielded from view by vegetation.

Cowboy had been parked there for a few hours when shuffling footsteps and the sound of someone slapping the side of the car with their hand woke him from a light doze. Suddenly someone placed their hands on the driver's side door and looked in at Cowboy. The man wore a grease-stained florescent orange baseball hat that advertised "The Pub." His fingernails were broken and dirty and he had open sores on the back of his hands. Cowboy immediately thought "meth head" and his guess was confirmed as the man began speaking rapidly, slurring his words, and exposing a mouth of rotten and missing teeth.

"Hey man. Waddayagotforme? Where's Junior? This the Chick Magnet. I knew it right off."

Looking into the back seat, the man grew suspicious.

"What the fuck? Where's Junior? You steal this car? This is the Chick Magnet man. Look. I can still see the name."

Moving his hands over the area where Cowboy had scraped off the words "Chick Magnet," the man leaned in the driver's side window.

"Hey fucker, Waddayagotforme?"

The meth head had recognized the car, appeared to know the original owner, and likely where he had lived - and where Cowboy was staying. He had also gotten a good close-up look at Cowboy. It was just bad luck – for Cowboy and definitely for the meth-head. What were the odds of running into someone who recognized the car from decades ago? Oh well, Cowboy thought. In a smooth, practiced movement he unsheathed the Ka-Bar combat knife and swung it in an arc across his body, jamming it into the base of the man's neck just above his clavicle. The knife went in smoothly, up to the hilt, and Cowboy pushed hard with it against the man's sagging body before he withdrew the blade. The man fell back into the bushes, and the bright pumping stream of arterial blood arced up and back, spraying the bushes next to the car as the meth-head disappeared into the vegetation. Cowboy looked in the rear-view mirror again – no one else was visible in the parking lot. Slipping the bloody Ka-Bar into the almost empty pretzel bag, he dropped it on the floor on the passenger side, leaned out the car's window to make sure no blood had spattered on the driver's door, and then drove slowly out of the lot.

15
EMMA
WEDNESDAY

Emma had called and made an appointment to interview Sheriff Hudson at eleven on Wednesday morning and had driven down to Dover-Foxcroft from Greenville in plenty of time. She decided to stop in at the Rite Aid Pharmacy beforehand to pick up a few things. Exiting the drug store with her purchases, she dropped them off in her car and then walked across the parking lot toward the sheriff's office. Emma paused at the cross street that ran between the drugstore and the sheriff's office and county court to let a black Honda drive by, and Cowboy looked directly at her from twenty feet away as he slowly passed in the Chick Magnet. Emma had never seen the man before but froze, drew a sharp breath, and felt her heart rate abruptly increase as she returned his stare. It was the same autonomic reaction that she had had the previous summer when she had turned a corner on the Appalachian Trail and come face to face with a large black bear that took a long look at her before shuffling off the path and down a steep embankment. Emma waited until Cowboy had driven out of sight before continuing across the street and climbing the stairs to the sheriff's office.

Sheriff Hudson came out from behind his desk to shake her hand, and with a puzzled expression, looked over her shoulder.

"No photographer? I figured you would want to take my picture for your profile of me."

"Sorry sheriff – no photographs. It's not really a profile, just some background questions for you. OK if I sit down?"

"Of course, have a seat."

Hudson looked surprisingly polished this morning, likely in anticipation that he would have his picture taken for a glowing profile in the Boston Globe. He had gotten a haircut from Andy, "The Barber," down the street at Sweet Lou's barbershop, and his uniform was clean and pressed, with nary a food stain to be seen. Now he was frowning, and as Emma set her recorder down on his desk and turned it on, her first question did not improve his mood.

"Sheriff, why aren't you cooperating with Detective Bateman's homicide investigation? Doesn't county law enforcement usually team up with the state police on such cases?"

Not taking his eyes off Emma's tight T-shirt, and apparently not noticing the tape recorder, the sheriff responded.

"Well honey, aren't you awfully young to be asking such questions? I don't know about other counties degree of cooperation with the state police, but we do, sometimes, but not always. Right now we have a really full plate with important ongoing investigations."

"What's more important than murder?"

Smiling now, leaning back and shifting his gaze up to meet Emma's stare, Hudson replied in a condescending tone.

"Well, decisions about manpower allocation can be quite complex – not something you could easily understand – lots of different variables involved."

"Why not give the job to Investigator Quinn? She did a great job teaming up with Detective Bateman on that serial murder case a while back."

"Little Annie? She actually played a small role in that investigation and had to be rescued from the killer. The media, like Bateman, were infatuated with her looks and inflated her role to make the story more dramatic. Unfortunately she believed some of the hype and has been puffing herself up ever since. I've put a stop to that though – she's handling things more appropriate to her gender and skill set now – domestic disputes and women's issues. And to be honest, I'm not sure she's really cut out for law enforcement."

"If she's such a poor performer, why have I heard rumors that Senator Collins has invited her to serve on a blue ribbon task force that's being formed down in Washington?"

Sitting forward now, placing his hands palms down on his desk, Hudson blustered.

"I haven't heard anything about that. I don't believe it. What task force?"

Smiling broadly, enjoying herself now, Emma let the silence build as she casually scratched her leg.

"Oh, I heard it has something to do with the struggles women face in traditionally male-dominated professions, like law enforcement. I'm surprised she hasn't mentioned the invitation to you. You will support her participation, won't you?"

Squinting, looking at Emma, then down at the recorder, Hudson carefully replied.

"My office is always pleased to contribute our expertise to any of the senator's initiatives."

"Do you think Investigator Quinn - 'Annie' as you call her, will bring much personal experience of difficulties in the workplace to the taskforce, Sheriff Hudson?"

Crossing his arms in a classic defensive body language gesture, Hudson frowned.

"We pride ourselves here in the sheriff's department on our support and encouragement of all minorities, including women and the disabled."

Clearly angry now, Hudson started to rise, indicating an end to the interview. A sudden commotion outside Hudson's office was followed by the appearance of Jim Torben in the doorway.

"Sheriff, you need to come next door to the Rite Aid – there's a body."

A small crowd had gathered at the rear of the Rite Aid parking lot and were trying to get a better look at a body hidden in the bushes – just a foot wearing a worn out sneaker could be seen projecting out over the curb. A uniformed sheriff's deputy who was trying to shoo people away looked relieved as Torben and Hudson pushed through the crowd, followed closely by Emma, who quietly started taking pictures of the foot, the assembled gawkers, and the police. Looking distinctly uncomfortable with being out of his office and actually involved, up close, in what appeared to be a crime – a killing, Hudson looked completely adrift as Jim Torben turned to him for instructions. Recognizing the blank expression on Hudson's face, Torben pulled him aside.

"Sheriff, maybe I should take charge of the investigation here while you return to the office and contact the state police through official channels. I'll secure the crime scene and get in touch directly with Detective Bateman, who can probably get here pretty quickly."

Hudson nodded.

"Torben, I am giving you complete authority on this – you contact Bateman and I will inform the Major Crime Unit in Bangor that you will be our man on the investigation – this is too close to home, and we need to be involved. Whatever you want, you got it. Any other people you need, you got em."

Resisting the urge to salute, Torben responded, "Yes sir," and watched as Hudson walked quickly back across the street and into the sheriff's office and courthouse.

Emma had overheard the exchange and approached Torben. She was going to tell him about the scary man in the black car she had seen drive away from the crime scene a short time ago, but then paused and decided not to. Maybe the man she saw was involved in the rapes. Maybe she could track him down on her own and get his story.

Emma hung around the parking lot for another hour or so, taking video she thought local TV news teams might want, until the evidence response team and Peter Martell arrived and started processing the crime scene. When the body was removed, she checked her watch and realized she would have to hurry if she was going to be on time for her meeting with George, Virginia Breen's brother. For some reason he had agreed to talk to her only on deep background, with no mention of his name, and in an out of the way location. They had agreed to meet by the Sebec Village Reading Room, right next to the dam, on the way up to the north shore of Sebec Lake.

She drove down the hill and around the corner into Sebec Village a few minutes late, and George was standing next to his car as she pulled up next to him. He hurriedly climbed in her car, looked at his watch, and then instructed her to turn right on a side road that followed the south shore of the river downstream from the dam. After a few hundred yards he said she could pull over, and she turned off the car and pulled out her recorder.

"No. No. No recording. No photos. No names. No record of this conversation ever took place. I'll tell you some things about my sister and her business dealings, and you'll retell the narrative that she and I agreed upon before her death – that she forced me out of the company, and I have absolutely no knowledge of what she was up to the last few years. Agreed?"

"Sure. I can do that. But why did you even agree to meet with me if I can't tell your story?"

"You are telling my story. And it's a story that will help to keep me alive. It's also a good story for you to embrace if you have any sense. I didn't want you poking around and maybe finding out something, or suggesting something in your articles, that might give people the wrong impression – that I know stuff I don't."

"O.K. So tell me the real story – what really happened between you and your sister?"

"Well, everything had been going great – business was good. Sis had a real gift for identifying properties that would increase in value over the near to mid-term, and we were making lots of money. And then purely by accident I stumbled on some documents that showed she had gotten herself involved in some big money dealings with questionable people and hadn't told me anything about it. I confronted her and she blew me off – saying if I was afraid of taking risks I could simply pretend I didn't know and take a back seat in what was being planned."

Emma nodded encouragement, and George took a deep breath and continued.

"She hadn't named any names but I already had a pretty good idea of the kind of people she was probably getting into business with, given the bank transfers out of Cyprus. So I told her I didn't want to be in the back seat or anywhere remotely close to the deal she was planning and I didn't want to know anything about it or the people involved. Not a thing. Nothing. She just laughed, and we agreed she would buy me out. It was a good deal for me – the terms were very generous, and I took the money and never looked back."

"What now?" Emma asked.

"Here's what happens now, Emma. You say in your articles that I left the company long before Virginia got involved in this activity, and you and I both get to live long healthy lives. These are not people to fool around with. Look what happened to my sister."

"But what's the deal she was getting into? Who were her business partners?"

"No. You don't want to know. I honestly don't know, and I wouldn't tell you if I did. My clear and sincere message to you is to steer clear of that line of inquiry. You won't learn much in any case, and you could put both of us at risk."

Disappointed that George had nothing to offer other than a vague warning about bad people, Emma dropped him off back at his car and started the hour drive back up to Greenville. Brushing aside his warnings, she was already thinking about how to try to get access to financial information about Virginia Breen's shady business deals.

As George got out of her car, a young Japanese woman, the same woman who she had encountered when she met Fred Williams at the Black Frog, snapped several pictures of Emma and George with a telephoto lens from her vantage point up the hill near the intersection with the Old Brownville Road.

Late that afternoon Jim Torben, Anne Quinn, and Doug Bateman settled into a booth at Alley Oops, the bar adjoining Pat's Pizza, a few blocks down the street from where the meth addict was stabbed to death. Ordinarily they would have used a conference room at the courthouse, but Torben wanted to avoid the possibility of encountering Sheriff Hudson. The bar was almost empty, so they didn't need to worry about being overheard. Jim Torben took a sip of his beer and began

"The sheriff wants to stay as far away from this as he can – but still be ready to step up to the podium if things go well. He's given me full authority to manage our side of the investigation, with the State Police of course taking the lead in the case, and is of course casting me in the scapegoat role if things don't go well. Which is fine with me.

The victims' name is Jack O'Connell. He grew up in the Greenville area but he's been living in Bangor the last few years. A meth addict, he has been in and out of jail for petty theft and public disturbances, and has had a few overdoses. Sheriff Hudson sees his killing as a drug deal gone wrong, but I don't think so. I can't see a drug deal taking place within fifty yards of the sheriff's office and in broad daylight. I think the Cowboy rapist was waiting for Anne so he could get another chance to kill her, and O'Connell somehow got in the way."

Doug checked his notes and jumped in.

"I agree Jim. I think it's the Cowboy. I got off the phone with my lieutenant a little while ago, and since I'm already up here he said I should add the O'Connell murder to my other cases, at least for the time being. And having the cooperation and participation of the county sheriff's office will be essential. Peter Martell and his crime scene crew didn't find any evidence of a struggle, or any dropped drugs or money. It looks like he was killed by a single stab wound that severed the carotid artery. A big knife and a strong, perfectly placed thrust –the killer knew what he was doing. Given the

Cowboy's prominent display of a big knife during his rapes, and his attempted assault at Anne's home, he gets my vote as the likely killer of O'Connell. So far we have no witnesses and no CCTV footage – the killer seems to have just disappeared." Looking at Anne, Doug continued.

"This guy is getting too close to Anne. I think we need to have around the clock protection for her until we catch him."

Anne looked ready to object but Jim Torben raised his hand and spoke first.

"That's exactly what we're going to do. She's going to have to start wearing a vest too. No discussion. Since we now have good reason to believe the Cowboy rapist is responsible for the killing of O'Connell, Anne's investigation of the rapes and your investigation of the killing today are linked, and the two cases should be combined and you two should work together. I also want to be involved as much as possible, and Doug, you need to ask for more help – maybe your partner Tom Richard can be assigned to help us."

Both men looked at Anne, and she nodded.

"Patty Crown, the FBI profiler I have been working with also urged me to get protection, so I'm OK with that, as long as I'm still actively involved in the search for this freak. Doug can cover the nights and I don't mind him staying close during the day, and when we are following different leads Jim or Tom can babysit me."

16
COWBOY
WEDNESDAY

Cowboy recognized the woman standing at the curb as he pulled away from the Rite Aid parking lot – it was the reporter who had been writing about the murders up at Moosehead – Emma something. He had seen her at the town hall meeting on the Lily Bay development and then a few times having breakfast at Auntie M's next to the Library in Greenville. She had just gotten a good look at him and the Chick Magnet, and as he slowed for the stop sign and turned right on Main, heading down past the Bangor Saving Bank and the Thompson Free Library, he knew he would have to make another change in vehicles, and soon. She could easily alert the local cops about the car. He had a plan for switching cars and headed out to Ladd Brothers Engineworks in Sebec Corners.

Cowboy was distracted as he turned left off Main at the Weber Hardware and then right by Brown's Mill, taking the River Road out past the cemetery and the Harry Oakes crypt. Emma, the reporter, he realized, looked a lot like Faith, a woman he had spent a lot of time with at the Waldo Christian Family compound back in New Mexico. Emma was taller and thinner than Faith, a lot younger, and didn't have a wandering eye, like Faith. But she had the same short black hair, oval face, and large hazel eyes. Faith had been the Cowboy's defender and mentor in the WCF, right from the start.

That first afternoon, when the Patriarch and his women - the "sisters," had picked him up along the side of a dirt road in west Texas, it hadn't taken the Patriarch long to start in on the Cowboy. Glancing sideways at him as they drove west toward the New

Mexico border, the Patriarch looked at the scrawny, filthy boy that he had named Enoch, so clearly neglected and abused, and wondered if he was up to what would be asked of him.

"Look at me boy. Can you put the baby?"

This elicited peals of laughter from the three sisters in the back seat. Enoch didn't answer – just looked confused and afraid. Seeing the boy's puzzled expression, Abraham the Patriarch tried again.

"Jesus, how stupid are you, son. Ever do any fuckin? Do you pleasure yourself? Do you stroke your cock?"

Enoch's neck reddened with embarrassment and he silently nodded.

"Do you squirt, boy? Do you squirt God's essence on the ground? Do you waste it?"

Before Enoch could respond, Faith leaned forward from her place in the middle of the back seat and slid her arms around his shoulders. Her arms were warm and comforting and she smelled good.

"Leave him be now. We can teach him everything. You'll see. Don't you worry none, we'll teach you how to put the baby, Enoch – I bet you're a real fast learner."

Cowboy turned north off the River Road onto Old Stagecoach Road, and when he had crossed over Route 6 at Sebec Corners he slowed and pulled in behind the Ladd Brothers Engineworks. There were easily fifty or so vehicles in various states of decay scattered across the lot behind the Ladd Brothers garage, most of them partially obscured by tall weeds and grass. Weaving between the wrecks, Cowboy drove the Chick Magnet in behind a small yellow school bus that was missing its engine but still carried the "Bowerbank" name on the side. He spent a few minutes carefully wiping down the inside and exterior of the car to make sure no fingerprints remained, removed the license plates and threw them deeper into the underbrush. Then he walked around to the front of the garage to look over their assortment of used pickup trucks and vintage cars for sale. A dark blue Ford 150 pickup with a $1,500 price tag painted on the windshield caught his attention, and after a quick test drive he paid in cash. The temporary plates on the truck were only good for thirty days but by then he would be long gone. Stopping off at the Sebec Country Store, Cowboy topped off the truck – its gas gauge didn't work, and bought a pair of sunglasses and a "Moxie" baseball hat. Driving back up Route 6 toward his hideout, Cowboy thought he would stop at Spring Creek BBQ in Monson for a late lunch before heading home to the Barn and a nice nap.

Enoch and Faith had become very close in the time he spent as a member in good standing of the Waldo Christian Family. She was the mother he never had, protecting him as best she could from the Patriarch's beatings, taking charge of his book learnin', and of course, introducing him to his new role as the font of God's essence. He was the source. Faith and the other half dozen or so women in the compound – the sisters, were the vessels – their number varied depending on the demands of their jobs in Santa Fe or down in Albuquerque. Together, the divine mission of Enoch and the sisters was to produce babies – blessed new members of the family of the faithful.

Enoch and the sisters of the Waldo Christian Family all shared a large barn-like structure with Enoch having his own room and the women sleeping in an open dormitory. The Patriarch had his own house, located on the other side of the run-down compound, across an open courtyard. The women in the WCF cleaned Abraham's house and his clothes and cooked his meals, but he had no carnal relations with them. He would lead them in prayer each morning before they set off to work and then again when they returned in the late afternoon, before the evening meal. After dinner they would have another, longer, candlelit service where Abraham would bless the conjugal union that was to take place that night between Enoch and one of the women in the family, asking God to bless them with a divine conception.

The first night, when they had arrived at the compound after a hard day's driving, Faith had drawn Enoch a bath and gently washed him clean with a cloth and sweet smelling soap. She had paid particular attention to his groin, and her gentle soapy stroking of his penis had yielded the expected result. She dried him off, led him to bed, and they slept in each other's arms. The next morning, early, Enoch was awoken by the touch of Faith's warm hands, and she showed him what was meant by the Patriarch's phrase "put the baby."

That same afternoon, under a bright New Mexican sun, the Patriarch joined Enoch and Faith in holy matrimony. For the first month that Enoch spent at the compound Faith shared his bed each night and he dutifully tried his best to plant God's seed. After his first month of exclusivity with Faith, Enoch was married in turn to each of the other women in the dormitory, and so began their nightly rotation through Enoch's bed.

Other than his nightly responsibility of sowing the divine essence, Enoch was not, at first, called on to do much around the compound. He was given instruction by the Patriarch in the mornings and then allowed to relax and study the bible in the afternoons. He took long naps, regained his strength, and gained weight. But as the months passed and none of the sisters was blessed with child, Enoch came under increasingly strict discipline from the Patriarch. His commitment to the faith was questioned. His morning instructions took on more of a physical nature – slaps to the side of the head when the Patriarch's questions were not quickly answered or his answers were deemed inadequate. The Patriarch's after dinner blessings became more perfunctory and the sisters began to tease Enoch and question his virility – maybe he was not the blessed font of divine seed. Maybe he was useless.

Then, eight months after his arrival at the compound – a miracle. One of the sisters – Eloise Baker, announced that she was with child. Her condition was confirmed by a home pregnancy test and Faith was given responsibility for managing her pre-natal care. The Patriarch did not permit any contact with the medical profession.

Her pregnancy reaffirmed Enoch's status as the font of divine essence, and the other sisters rededicated themselves to receiving God's seed through Enoch, his anointed disciple.

In a candlelit procession the newly pregnant Eloise was led across the courtyard and joined Abraham in his house, beginning her blessed confinement. She would not leave the compound until after the child was born, and except for the evening meal she was rarely seen outside Abraham's house. Her full-term pregnancy was uneventful and surrounded by Faith and her other sisters she was delivered of a healthy baby girl in the house of the Patriarch.

Abraham baptized the child and named her Esther. He proclaimed that she was under his divine protection and would be raised under his roof, but he soon tired of the noise and disruption. Within a few weeks Esther and her mother had moved back across the courtyard into the house that Enoch shared with the sisters of the Waldo Christian Fellowship of Heaven and Earth.

The fortunes of the WCF slowly deteriorated over the next several years. There was some turnover - a few new sisters were recruited into the family and a few simply disappeared – going off to work one day and never returning. Enoch fathered only two more children, by Faith and by Eloise. These additions to his flock pleased the Patriarch, but suspicions grew among some of the sisters that had not become pregnant that Enoch might not be the father of the new babies of the WCF. Both Eloise and Faith, they suspected, may have found other men from outside the family to father their children, both to protect Enoch from further beatings from the Patriarch and also to increase their own status within the family.

Abraham eventually came to share these suspicions and Enoch was removed from his privileged position and relegated to a much diminished status and role within the WCF. He no longer lay with the sisters and his major role now was as an example for the other members of the WCF - the Patriarch would occasionally give him an after-dinner beating as a lesson for the sisters. Enoch's days were now spent doing odd jobs when he could find them in the nearby town of Cerrillos. The Patriarch took over the responsibility of sowing the divine seed and several times a week he would visit the sister's dormitory and select one of them to join him in Enoch's old room. Enoch's nights were spent sleeping in an unused dog kennel behind the Patriarch's house. He didn't think it was too bad, as he had plenty of blankets for the cold nights and Faith would occasionally visit him and share his bed. He continued to hope that he would someday regain the faith of the Patriarch.

He was alone in his dog kennel on the cold November night the Santa Fe County Sheriff's deputies and New Mexico State Police raided the compound. Apparently one of the run-away sisters had told the authorities lurid tales of an old man running a cult and having sex with underage girls in a remote location. Unfortunately for Abraham the raid occurred on one of the evenings he was sowing divine seed, and they interrupted him fornicating with a recent arrival – a fourteen-year-old runaway from a prominent Santa Fe Family.

The authorities didn't quite know what to make of Enoch or what to do with him. When sheriff's deputies discovered him huddled on a bare mattress in a dirt-floored dog kennel they assumed him to be a victim – another weak-willed innocent swept up in the Patriarch's cult. His victim profile was further strengthened when it was learned that he had been abducted several years earlier while walking along a back road in Texas, and that his earlier life was a blank slate. Enoch did not remember, or chose not to recount, either his real name or really any aspects of his upbringing prior to joining the WCF, other than to say he moved around a lot as a kid. He could read and write but seemed to have had little if any formal education, and his limp, along with evidence of broken bones and numerous beatings, indicated a long history of physical abuse by the Patriarch and likely before. He was found to be fluent in Spanish and was familiar with many of the idioms associated with the Rio Grande borderlands – which would turn out playing a big role in the next phase of his life.

Enoch's relative isolation from the world and his lack of an early history or identity initially presented a problem for local and state authorities responsible for his care and management, but a solution was soon found that appealed to all concerned, including Enoch. He was enlisted into the US Army, and given his lack of any family ties or indeed any personal history at all, was identified as an excellent candidate for a newly formed hybrid program designed to facilitate greater cooperation and integration between the military and other governmental agencies.

Enoch quickly adapted to life in the military and he flourished during the brutal ten weeks of basic training he completed in the summer heat and humidity of Ft. Polk, Louisiana. Basic training was followed by another 10 weeks of advanced training in close quarters combat, along with CIA taught tradecraft courses in surveillance, establishing alternative identities, and blending into a range of different cultural environments. Enoch was also given a battery of personality tests that revealed both a lack of emotional attachment or empathy and a somewhat disturbingly casual approach to physical violence – traits that drew the attention of his instructors.

When his training was completed Enoch was transferred to a small unit being formed to assist the Department of Homeland Security in infiltrating and breaking up the "coyote" gangs that were smuggling illegal immigrants across the U.S. border with Mexico. For the next two years he drifted along the borderlands from Brownsville to Tijuana, moving between communities on both sides of the border, changing his identity and his appearance along the way, and getting close enough to coyote networks to identify the major players for Homeland Security. Once his targets had been identified and profiled, usually from a safe distance, Enoch would move on to the next assignment along the border, never staying in one location for more than a few weeks or so.

He was remarkably successful in his undercover activities and thoroughly enjoyed his work, particularly since it gave him enough free time to begin again with efforts to sow his divine seed with both willing and unwilling partners. His fervent hope was to rejoin the

Waldo Christian Family and to prove himself worthy to the Patriarch, who had been released from jail and had returned to the compound to start again – this time under the watchful eye of local law enforcement.

After about a year of simply identifying the major actors in coyote networks from a safe distance, Enoch's role changed as his handlers began to drift off script and he was directed, on his own initiative, to take more direct and conclusive actions to reduce the level of human smuggling across the border. Enoch was essentially tasked with the removal of key individuals in the coyote networks and given carte blanche in terms of how he carried out his mission. This program of unofficial targeted assassinations of what were considered "bad hombres" went well for several months, until Enoch inadvertently killed an undercover DEA agent in an incident just outside Nogales. The agent had worked his way into a position of trust within a major smuggling cartel and made the mistake of attempting to intervene as Enoch, knife drawn, was closing on his intended target – the cartel's second in command.

Needless to say, Enoch's killing of a DEA agent in a cantina outside of Nogales, and the attention it drew to their below the radar anti-coyote initiative, did not sit well with DHS upper management. It was decided that the best course of action would be to quietly separate him from government employment. At the same time, however, there was considerable pride in how well Enoch had performed, both because of his talent as a chameleon infiltrator, and for his skill in dispatching bad guys. Soon after his discharge from the army a private consulting firm that offered specialized services to a range of corporate clients hired Enoch. He made a smooth transition into the private sector, and quickly became a much sought after problem solver.

Enoch, aka Jimmy Bob Lentz, aka The Cowboy, had successfully carried out assignments in many parts of the country before coming to Maine. His previous jobs had varied considerably in duration and he was never sure how long each one would take. As he pulled his new Ford 150 pickup truck into the drive leading to his hideout south of Greenville, his phone buzzed with a text message. He read the single phrase that appeared on the screen – "final task," and realized his stay in Maine was almost over. The text message alerted him to an incoming encrypted email, and as soon as he reached his desk he opened his computer and downloaded the new file, which consisted of a photograph of a smiling middle-aged man, a name, and an address. Cowboy printed out the file and then wiped it from his computer. Stepping over to the bed, he knelt and reached under it, pushing aside his matrimonial ceremony pack, and slid out a vintage axe with "Merrill" written on the handle. Running his thumb along the rusty blade, Cowboy thought it would be nice to give it a good sharp cutting edge. As he stepped out of his RV and walked over to the workbench to sharpen the axe, he thought about what he should do – complete his assignment and leave Maine or try to add one more wife before he left – either Anne, who was still a strong challenge, or maybe Emma, whom he thought would be an easy conquest.

17
DOUGLAS
THURSDAY

Anne, Doug, and Jim Torben sat around a large wooden table in the county courthouse office that had been set aside for their now combined investigation of Cowboy's rapes and his suspected killing of the meth addict the previous day in the Rite Aid parking lot next door. Doug checked the time. Tom Richard was running a good twenty minutes late for their nine AM meeting. Doug hoped it was because he had decided to stop in Milo on his way up from the Maine State Police Barracks in Bangor to pick up donuts and coffee from Elaine's Café and Bakery.

Anne and Doug were both on edge – concerned that Sheriff Hudson would intervene to block the combining of the investigation of the rapes and the Rite Aid murder, even though Jim Torben had assured them that Hudson had given him complete oversight and responsibility for the joint investigation. Torben too, appeared anxious, however, and kept looking at his watch and over his shoulder at the open door to the hallway.

Hearing the sound of a closing door and footsteps in the hall, Anne looked up and smiled as Tom came into view carrying a box of Elaine's donuts and four coffees. Tom entered the office, put the donuts and coffees down on the table, and gave them a broad smile.

"Sorry I'm late. I stopped for donuts and then to join up with these two guys here in the parking lot."

Standing behind Tom were two men in suits. Both had somber expressions, and simply nodded a greeting. Jim visibly relaxed when he saw the two men accompanying Tom and replied to their nodded greeting.

"I'm certainly glad to finally see you two here."

Tom saw Doug and Anne's puzzled expressions and let out a quiet chuckle.

"We've got a few surprises for you this morning. Follow us for the first one."

Turning, Tom left the office and continued down the hall at a casual pace, followed closely by the two suited strangers. Reaching the door to Sheriff Hudson's office, Tom waited for Anne, Doug, and Jim to catch up and then entered without knocking. The sheriff was busy reading the Piscataquis Observer and eating a large bear claw pastry. He was clearly irritated at the interruption, brushed crumbs from his shirtfront, and started to speak, then stopped as he saw the two suits take up position in front of his desk. He stood as they reached inside their coats for IDs and looked confused as Tom Richard nonchalantly moved behind his desk to stand next to him, and then placed his hand over Hudson's holstered handgun. The older of the two suits broke the silence.

"Sheriff Hudson, I'm special agent Flannery with the FBI. This is special agent Evans. We are arresting you on a number of federal charges and are here to take you into custody. We have a car downstairs to transport you down to Boston." Agent Flannery continued addressing Hudson – reading him his Miranda rights and asking him to step away from behind his desk. Hudson twisted away from Tom, who slipped Hudson's handgun out of its holster and stepped back as the federal agents closed in to cuff the sheriff. Leading Hudson out of the office, the senior FBI agent smiled at Anne and thanked her for her help with the case. Anne frowned in puzzlement at the remark, and Hudson scowled at her as he shuffled down the hall and out of her life.

They followed Jim Torben back to the conference room and as the box of Elaine's donuts and the coffees were passed around, he filled them in on the arrest.

"Sorry to have kept you mostly in the dark on this but the feds wanted it that way. They have been looking at Hudson since before he won the election and building a case for his involvement with organized crime down in Boston. I had my own suspicions, which I shared with the FBI field office in Boston several months ago, and that's when I was drawn into the investigation."

Turning to Anne, Torben continued.

"Anne, your photos from over at Lagrange of our former sheriff meeting up with a high-level Boston mobster were a welcome addition to their case against him. I was glad to see they thanked you for that. They also wanted me to let you know that you will most likely be called to testify at trial."

Anne nodded.

"It will be my distinct pleasure."

Doug set his coffee down and asked.

"What was he involved in – drugs?

Torben nodded.

"Ayup. Mostly he was facilitating the movement of opioids and other drugs into Maine but may also have been active in other criminal enterprises being run out of Boston. The feds are curious as to why he was so concerned about keeping Anne away from any participation in Doug's murder cases up at Moosehead. We still don't have a clear idea of why he was blocking that – if it was just jealousy, or if there was more to it.

The good news is that I have been asked to take over as acting sheriff in the interim until the next election, and in that capacity am formally detailing Anne to all of your murder cases, Doug. County law enforcement needs to be involved, and you two make a good investigative team. I realize that's a lot to ask, and the rape cases will probably have to be set aside for now, as the homicides take precedence."

Setting down his second donut, Tom Richard opened a folder he had placed on the table and looked at Torben.

"If I may interject here. I mentioned earlier that there would be a few surprises this morning. A crooked sheriff was the first, and the second is in the folder here. It's the first DNA results back from the lab looking for matches to the samples recovered from the axe handle in the Virginia Breen killing. There is no match to the Potter killing – lots of DNA from Emma Lange at the Potter murder site, which is not surprising, but nothing else. But they did find a match with samples from two other crime scenes, which was somewhat of a surprise." Tom Richard paused for effect before continuing.

"The DNA from the Breen murder scene, recovered from the handle of the axe that split her skull, matches semen samples recovered from the rapes of both Betsy Crawford and Gayle Robertson. It certainly looks like your serial rapist, the Cowboy who brands his victims, is also killing people with axes."

Tom smiled at the surprised looks that greeted his news and continued.

"I think it's safe to say that things just got a lot simpler. We have a single perp and so far we can link him to two rapes, a botched rape attempt at Anne's, and two murders. All we have to do now is catch him."

Anne nodded and continued Tom's line of reasoning. "Actually that makes some sense. Patty Crown, the FBI profiler who has been searching databases nationally for rapes like the Crawford and Robertson assaults – with branding and marriage ceremonies, has found a pattern of numerous isolated clusters of rapes in different parts of the country. The rapes – two or three or more per cluster, occur over a pretty short period of time, then the rapist – we call him the Cowboy, vanishes, only to pop up somewhere else, often at a considerable distance, and carries out another cluster. What if the Cowboy is a contract killer? He moves around the country – wherever his job takes him, and the rapes are carried out on the side – like a hobby. I'll let Patty Crown, the profiler, know what we've learned, and ask her to look at the rape clusters she has identified and see if there are any unsolved murders that happened in the same areas at about the same time. I've already sent her our DNA results from the Cowboy rapes here and she's checking to see if there are any matches with the other rape clusters she's identified."

"While you're doing that," Jim Torben replied, "we'll be looking at the CCTV footage from Main Street. Rite Aid has a camera by the front door – it doesn't cover the back of the lot where the killing occurred but should show all the vehicles leaving the parking lot around the time of the murder. We might be able to get some footage of the car the killer was driving. There's also a camera east on Main at the Bangor Saving Bank, which could also provide some footage."

"A vehicle ID would be key," Doug commented. "He seems to know the area pretty well but he or his vehicle might be noticed if we get the word out and assign some cars to monitor the main roads. We also should ask the FBI to question Hudson about the Cowboy. If he knows he's now a person of interest in a murder investigation he might start talking."

Tom joined the conversation.

"We should also be checking local B&Bs, motels, and longer-term rentals between Dexter and Greenville, along with RV parks and camping areas – this Cowboy guy has to be hunkered down somewhere. It's a big area with lots of places to hide, but outsiders will certainly stand out."

Anne then interjected.

"We may not have much time to catch him before he pulls up stakes and disappears. We don't know how many people he has on his kill list, or who they are. He may already be on his way out of town."

"I don't think so," countered Doug. "He was staked out in the Rite Aid parking lot for a reason – likely targeting Anne at the sheriff's office. So he may just be hoping to add her to his current list of local brides before he vanishes. But I think there is another name on his hit list that he hasn't gotten to yet – or we haven't found yet. The CCTV footage from Kamp Kamp shows him buying two axes – one of which was used in the Virginia Breen murder, but the second axe, with "Merrill" on the handle, is still out there."

"I'm going to go back over all the business dealings of Potter and

Breen," Tom offered. "Maybe I missed their connection – the shared interest that whomever has hired the Cowboy wanted to snuff out. The Lily Bay project seems like the most likely commonality but maybe it's something else entirely."

"Sounds like we finally have some traction on this case," Doug said. "I'll start working with Jim on searching motels and other rentals for where he's staying and setting up some active monitoring of major roads. Let's meet back here at five to see where we are."

Anne returned to her desk and immediately called Patty Crown.

"Hi Patty. I've got an update from this end on the Cowboy, and a request."

"Anne. I was just about to call you. I also have some news. The DNA profile for the Cowboy from the two rapes up there that you sent to us are a match for at least two of the rape clusters in other parts of the country – the one in Virginia and the Park City cluster. I expect that others will also match. It looks like our Cowboy has been at this for quite a while - moving around a lot, and only staying in any one place for pretty short periods of time."

Anne replied. "We're also getting DNA linkage between cases. Semen samples from the two rapes were recently matched with a DNA sample recovered from one of the killings up here. We think Cowboy may be a contract killer – moving around the country on assignments, and that the rapes might be a hobby of sorts he conducts on the side. Can you go back and take another look at the rape clusters and see if there are any as yet unsolved murders in the same time frame – particularly prominent business leaders? Both of our murder victims had some sketchy business dealings and may have been targeted because of their opposition to a big development project up here."

"Sure thing," replied Patty. "That should be pretty easy. I'll get back to you tomorrow at the latest."

Anne still hadn't heard back from Patty Crown when they reconvened back around the conference table at five o'clock. Jim Torben led off with the results of the CCTV search.

"We found something right off on the Rite Aid camera covering the front of the parking lot," he commented. "I've got it loaded up here on the computer." Starting the first video clip, Jim described what they were looking at. "This first footage shows a beat-up Honda Accord – painted a dull black, parking across Main Street right after Anne arrives at the courthouse this morning. There's only the driver in the car. Can't see him too well at first but in the second clip – here, he exits the car and walks across Main and into the Rite Aid. He takes care, it seems, to shield his face from the camera. Here he is inside the store, and at the cash register, and then walking back out to the car. I think this is our guy."

Pausing to start the next clip, Jim continues.

"An hour or so later he moves the car from his parking place on Main into the Rite Aid parking lot, moving out of view toward the back of the lot where the killing took place."

Jim Torben set up the final clip.

"This footage is time-stamped 10:45 AM, which would be right around when we think the killing occurred in the back of the lot. Again, this is the Rite Aid camera at the front of the parking lot. You can see a woman exiting the drug store, crossing the parking lot toward the courthouse and then pausing on the sidewalk as the black Honda slowly cruises by her. The driver of the Honda looks directly at her from maybe fifteen feet away as he passes her, then turns right on Main. The Bangor Saving Bank camera picks up the car a little later as it proceeds on Main. Unfortunately we can't pick up the license number of the car so all we have is make and color and approximate year – not a lot to go on."

Tom Richard asked the obvious question.

"Any idea what the identity is of the eye witness who saw him close-up in that last clip?"

Doug responded immediately.

"I'm not sure but I think that's the reporter – Emma Lange."

Anne agreed.

"Yes, that's her. She's on her way to the courthouse for an eleven o'clock appointment with Hudson. He was bragging about being profiled for the Boston Globe."

"That's weird," Jim Torben added. "She was taking lots of pictures at the murder scene and interviewing people. I would have thought she would have mentioned seeing what might have been the killer close up. I can't imagine she didn't connect the car driving away with the killing."

"Maybe she wants to keep what she knows quiet for now and work it into one of her articles," Anne suggested. "Who knows? But we need to get to her quick – Cowboy has probably read her articles and seen her around and knows who she is. He might well go after her since she's an eye witness who can place him at the crime scene."

Doug agreed.

"I'll call Chief Marcus in Greenville and have him start the search for her. We've also got six county and state police units on the main roads from Newport down on the interstate up to Greenville – I'll get the description of the black Honda out to them with a warning to stop but to wait for backup before approaching – Cowboy is no doubt armed and extremely dangerous."

Looking down at his notes, Doug continued.

"Chief Marcus and some deputies here in the sheriff's office have been calling local motels, B&Bs, and other rentals, but with no good leads so far. They have also started checking with local realtors about longer-term rentals. It's also possible Cowboy found something without going through a normal business channel – finding a place on Craigslist or newspaper ads. Tracking those down will take a lot longer. Let's hope we get lucky."

Anne's phone rang and seeing that the call was from Patty Crown, she held her hand up, mouthed "FBI," and answered.

"Hi Patty. Did you find anything?

"Bull's-eye, Anne. The first three of the Cowboy's rape clusters that I checked on all had unsolved killings in the same area and time frame, and all three were business people. Your hunch was a good one – Cowboy could very likely be a contract killer with a wide geographical reach and a penchant for rapes on the side. I've notified higher-ups of the patterns and your ongoing investigation – we might be sending some reinforcements your way."

Anne thanked Patty and ended the call, assuring her that she would keep her in the loop as things developed. She relayed what Patty had told her and was somewhat surprised by the less than enthusiastic response from her colleagues. All three men frowned, and Tom explained.

"Getting the feds involved is a double-edged sword – they bring lots of resources and manpower to bear, but at the same time they usually impose a centralized top-down organizational structure that translates into locals getting pushed to the margins and having little say in how the investigation is carried out."

Doug nodded.

"Let's hope we can catch this guy before the feds get too involved. We have the black car lead, and Emma Lange as a potential eyewitness. Finding her is our top priority right now, before Cowboy does."

18
ANNE
FRIDAY

Anne and Doug walked in the front door of Spencer's Bakery and Cafe in Dover-Foxcroft a little after eight AM and joined Jim Torben in a booth by the front window. After breakfast Jim and Anne were going to head up to Greenville and join Chief Marcus in ongoing efforts to track down Emma Lange, who was not answering her phone and had not been seen at the Black Frog since yesterday. Doug would be driving down to Bangor to provide a briefing on the case for Captain Shetler, the commanding officer of Major Crime Units North.

The other customers paid scant attention to Anne and Doug – the novelty of them being a couple had faded, and so far news of the intensified investigation into Cowboy's string of murders and rapes had not leaked out. The arrest of Sheriff Hudson had also not yet become public, and they hoped that it wouldn't hit the press until next Monday when he was arraigned. Jim Torben, as the acting sheriff, would be in the hot seat then, and he was already making preparations for a press conference on Monday afternoon. He had invited Captain Shetler, Doug's boss, to co-host it with him. As Jim talked over the plans for the press conference with Doug and Anne, they both thought they were seeing the beginning of his campaign for sheriff, and hoped he would be on the ballot in the coming fall election.

An hour's drive north of Spencer's Cafe where Anne, Doug, and Jim were having breakfast, Bob Whallon and George Peebles were pulling into the parking lot where the east outlet of the Kennebec

River flowed out of Moosehead Lake. Theirs was the only vehicle in the lot. Bob and George decided to work the north side of the shallow rock-strewn river, and Whallon headed downstream toward Indian Pond. A retired university professor, he had been an avid fly fisherman since his youth, and still had some of the flies he had tied as a teenager. Tall and taciturn, he enjoyed the solitude and silence of the Kennebec, and quickly lost sight of Peebles as he moved downstream in what was shaping up to be a beautiful summer day in northern Maine. Even though he had poor luck, catching just a single brown trout that did not meet the minimum length requirement, Whallon thoroughly enjoyed the morning, and three hours passed quickly.

Working his way back upriver toward the parking lot, he was surprised when he didn't see Peebles, and wondered if he had decided to move upstream under the Route 6 Bridge and the railroad bridge toward the dam. Whallon stopped at the parking lot, took off his waders and locked his fishing gear in the truck before continuing upstream to search for Peebles. Almost a half-hour later, after walking the north bank of the river all the way to the dam looking for his fishing companion, Whallon reluctantly pulled out his cell phone and called for help. He and George had joked over breakfast that morning that since Peebles had been involved in business deals with both Richard Potter and Virginia Breen, they should be on the lookout for anyone carrying an axe.

The 911 call from Whallon was routed to the Greenville Police, and the dispatcher patched it through to Chief Marcus, who was having lunch at the Black Frog with Anne and Jim. They had spent the morning checking Emma Lange's room upstairs at the Black Frog and canvassing the town for her, with no luck. From their table on the dock they could see the empty parking space in the Moosehead Marine Museum lot where Emma usually left her car, near where the steamship Katahdin docked and took on passengers for cruises around Sugar Island and up to Mt. Kineo.

The report of a missing fly fisherman didn't register with Chief

Marcus initially, until Whallon mentioned that his fishing buddy George Peebles had been involved in business deals with both Potter and Breen. Marcus abruptly interrupted Whallon in mid-sentence.

"Stay right there Professor Whallon. We are on our way to you and will be there in twenty minutes. Keep looking."

Chief Marcus brought Anne and Jim up to speed as they hurried to Anne's Land Cruiser and headed northwest out of town. Peebles could well already be dead, they knew, tied to a tree somewhere along the Kennebec River, but Anne and Jim called to set up roadblocks to the north and south along Route 6 in the hope he had been abducted by the Cowboy and might still be alive. Not knowing how much of a head start Cowboy might have, Jim checked first with the Somerset County Sheriff's Office over in Madison, but they did not have a patrol car at the north end of the county that afternoon. His second call was to the U. S Border Patrol Office in Jackman, and they immediately agreed to screen all northbound vehicles along route 6 and also to send a car over to the junction of Route 6 and the Northern Road in case Cowboy chose to head straight north out of Rockwood into the wilderness and then around the Golden Road. While Jim was setting up roadblocks north along Route 6, Anne called the Piscataquis Sheriff's Office and ordered one set up to stop southbound vehicles in Monson, about an hour south of where Peebles had gone missing. Along with the general description they had of Cowboy, the roadblocks were given instructions to be particularly on the lookout for a black Honda Accord and to approach all vehicles with heightened caution – Cowboy being considered armed and extremely dangerous.

Whallon was waiting in the parking lot when they arrived and after hearing his account of the morning's fishing timeline and his brief search for Peebles, Chief Marcus called down to Greenville to arrange for volunteers to begin a more systematic search of both sides of the Kennebec. Whallon reaffirmed that he was downstream of Peebles the entire morning and confident that he would have seen him if he had lost his footing, swamped his waders, and been carried away by the current.

Anne, Jim, and Chief Marcus joined Whallon in another, more systematic, search of the north bank of the river from the dam downstream as far as Whallon had gone that morning, with no luck. Then, as they neared the parking lot again, Jim saw something in a shallow ditch, reached down, and held a fly rod aloft. Whallon confirmed that it was Peebles's Orvis rod, and not something that would be casually discarded, given its price tag of almost a thousand dollars. A second, even more disturbing find was made when Anne walked across the bridge to survey the south shore of the river. Toward the middle of the span on the southbound side a double bladed axe with "Merrill" printed on the handle lay at the edge of the pavement next to a large pothole where the concrete had collapsed, giving a view of the river below through now exposed rebar. The axe had damage to the handle where it had hit the side of the bridge and pavement, perhaps when it had bounced out of a vehicle. The absence of blood on the blade of the axe and its location in the middle of the bridge, along with the recovered fly rod, suggested that Peebles may have been abducted and taken south over the bridge, and might still be alive.

The search volunteers started arriving about an hour later, and Jim and Anne decided to return to Greenville and continue looking for Emma Lange, leaving Chief Marcus to organize the expanded search for Peebles. The roadblocks were called off. Emma had not been seen at the Kamp Kamp store, Auntie M's, the Black Frog, or the other businesses they checked in Greenville, so Anne and Jim continued south on Route 6, back to Dover-Foxcroft.

Passing through the town of Monson, around the curve and up the hill toward the Civil War memorial, they were both surprised when a black Honda Accord pulled out and passed them in a no passing zone, accelerating up the hill and going at least twenty miles over the posted speed limit. Anne turned on the siren and strobe light bar behind the grill on her Toyota and after a brief chase, the Honda slowed and pulled to a complete stop on the shoulder. Anne pulled up several cars lengths behind the Honda and she and Jim both exited the Toyota but remained crouched behind the protection provided by the vehicle's doors, weapons drawn and leveled on the Honda.

Before either of them could call out any orders, the driver's side door flew open and the driver stepped out and faced them.

"Oh for Christ's sake," Anne muttered, and Jim added an angry "Shit." Both recognized David Meltz, a fourteen-year-old from Sebec Village who had built up quite a reputation over the past several years for stealing cars and going on joy rides. David waved and walked toward them with a sheepish look on his face.

"Hi Jim, hi Anne. Sorry for the crazy passing and stuff." Laughing he added, "But I don't get driver's training till next year."

Seeing their drawn weapons and tense expressions, Meltz stopped smiling. Once he was cuffed and in the back of the Toyota and a tow truck had been called, Anne and Jim took a closer look at the Honda. It certainly looked like the car they had seen in the Rite Aid CCTV footage, and the fine spray of blood that was still visible on the driver's door supported their suspicions. When told that the car he was driving had been involved in a murder, Meltz quickly told his story on the drive down to Dover-Foxcroft.

He and his friend Don Gray had been searching through the field of discarded vehicles behind Ladd Brother's Engineworks in Sebec Corners on Thursday night, hoping to find hubcaps or other items that could be sold on Craigslist or eBay, when they saw the Honda hidden in the tall grass behind the Bowerbank school bus. The keys were still in the ignition and when it started right up, David figured it was like finding an abandoned ship adrift at sea and that the Honda was his for the taking. He had been driving it on back roads all day and had just pulled onto Route 6 when they caught him. He had no idea who had left the car behind the school bus and hadn't seen anyone else around the field of rusting vehicles.

Meltz was handed over to the Division of Juvenile Services and Anne and Jim turned their attention to the Honda and where David had found it. The state police evidence response team was called and would be going over the vehicle looking for fingerprints and DNA, along with any other relevant evidence. Anne conducted a quick search of the Honda, now secure in a fenced enclosure behind the courthouse, and turned up nothing other than the diet Coke bottle and empty pretzel bag Cowboy had forgotten on the floor behind the driver's seat. Both would be good potential sources for DNA and prints. The VIN number plates on the dashboard, driver's door jam, and firewall had all been removed, so they would have to wait on the evidence response team's search for the hidden VIN number locations to begin tracking the vehicle's ownership history.

Anne decided to take a look at where David claimed to have found the Honda and arrived at the Sebec Corners and Ladd Brother's Engineworks a little after five PM. The front doors were locked and the interior was dark. The front lawn displayed several dozen used vehicles for sale – some rusted vintage and others more recent in age. Anne walked around the side of the building, looking for the Bowerbank school bus in the back lot. She saw an older man walking from the rear door of the building toward his car.

"Excuse me – sir – do you work here?"

"Sure do. I'm Dennis. Dennis Walker. What can I do for you, miss?"

Anne introduced herself as she approached Dennis, who glanced at his watch before shaking her hand.

"A black Honda was stolen from your back lot a few days ago. It was parked next to the school bus. I'm wondering what you can tell me about it."

Walker laughed before responding

"Not much chance of that – unless they towed it away. Nothing back there runs anymore – we call it the cemetery."

"Well, we think it was abandoned back there on Wednesday –

the day before yesterday. Don't you don't know anything about how it got there?"

"Nope. Never saw it. I rarely go back there."

"Anyone else who might have seen it or the person who left it there?"

"Well... Maybe George. He was also working Wednesday."

"How can I contact him?"

Reaching for his phone, Dennis replied.

"He left a few hours ago - got a jump on the weekend. Going fishing up at First Roach Pond I think. I can give you his phone number."

"Thanks. Just one more question Dennis. Did you sell any vehicles on Wednesday? Maybe the person who dumped the car out back was in the market for something used."

Dennis paused and then smiled and nodded.

"Come on back inside – I think you might be right. I sold a Ford pickup to a guy Wednesday afternoon. He just walked in and bought it after a short test drive. Paid cash - fifteen hundred dollars. It was a little weird."

Anne followed Dennis back into the office and collected all the paperwork for the sale, slipping it into plastic evidence envelopes. The description of the buyer – Jimmy Bob Lentz - medium height, short reddish blond hair, slight limp – was a good match for the Cowboy, which meant they should be looking for a dark blue Ford 150 pickup. She called Jim Torben and Tom Richard as she drove back to Dover-Foxcroft and they both got started on getting alerts out on the truck. Jim told her the evidence response team had located the hidden VIN number on the Honda, stamped into the frame behind the catalytic converter, and they had identified the owner of record – James Price.

The car had not been registered for five years, ever since Price had been caught in a meth lab raid and sentenced to five years in the Maine State Prison down in Warren. He was paroled several years ago and had moved to Springfield Massachusetts. They were still trying to contact him and the local police in Springfield were checking his residence and workplace. Jim Torben added that they might just have what they needed, even before locating Price, since his address as listed on the last vehicle registration for the Honda was a rural location off Route 6 up between Shirley and Greenville. It was apparently a farm that had been in the Price family for generations but was now vacant. Maybe that's where Cowboy had been living for the last month and where he had taken George Peebles.

Doug was due back from Bangor in a few minutes and Jim had already called Chief Marcus in Greenville and asked him to meet them in Shirley and to bring as many officers as were available. As soon as Anne and Doug arrived back in Dover-Foxcroft they would head up to Shirley with Jim and several of his sheriff's deputies. State Police cruisers that were in the area would also meet them in Shirley, and patrol cars were again positioned on Route 6 north of Greenville and in Monson to watch for the blue Ford pickup.

It was dark by the time Doug Bateman started handing out instructions to the dozen or so law enforcement personnel who had assembled in Shirley for the raid on the Price farm. They would drive down the side road off Route 6 and then continue in on foot when they reached the long drive leading to the farm. There was no SWAT team among the dozen men gathered around Doug, but they had all grown up hunting, most were combat veterans, and many carried semiautomatic rifles. Tom Richard had already gone ahead to recon the farmhouse and barn and would be reporting back to them once he was in position. He had done a lot of Special Forces recon during his military service and since joining the state police was often called on in situations like this to take a first look at things before operations were initiated.

Tom had advanced almost to the farmhouse by the time the police vehicles had parked at the end of the driveway. He had not yet seen any evidence of surveillance cameras, motion sensors, or other indications that the Cowboy had been or was currently at the farm. He cautiously circled the farmhouse and was confident that it had not been occupied for a considerable period of time. Crouching down at a corner of the house, Tom turned his attention to the barn and immediately noticed a number of indicators that it was in current use - tire tracks of several different vehicles could be seen in the open area leading up to the barn doors, and there were broad scraped areas in the dirt where the barn doors had been opened. Pulling out his night vision scope Tom noted the CCTV camera mounted at the peak of the roof as well as the new lock on the smaller entry door to the barn. Talking quietly into his radio, he reported back to Doug.

"I think we have something here. The farmhouse is clear – unoccupied. But the barn is locked up tight and has at least one surveillance camera. I can't tell if anyone is in there but the driveway is clear – you can come on up and we'll decide what's next."

Tom had stepped out from behind the corner of the farmhouse and was starting to move toward the barn when he was knocked to the ground by the shock wave as the barn exploded in a large fireball. Looking up from his position on the ground he could clearly see the interior of the barn, which now lacked a roof and two of its walls. It appeared to be empty except for three burning vehicles parked in a back corner – two pickup trucks and a compact car. Tom called Doug on the radio –

"Doug. Stay off the driveway – there might be IEDs. I'm not sure if I triggered something or if it was on a timer, but the barn just went up. I can see three vehicles burning inside but not much else. I think he was here but we missed him."

19
EMMA
FRIDAY – SATURDAY

The first calls and texts from Anne Quinn had started popping up on Emma Lange's phone as she was eating dinner Thursday night at the Black Frog, confirming what Emma had feared – the police had viewed the CCTV footage from the Rite Aid camera and now knew that she had seen the killer up close when he drove past her on the way out of the drugstore parking lot. Emma didn't want to talk to the police, and had turned off her phone in case they were trying to trace its location. She still hoped that she could contact the Cowboy and get his story before he was caught, and had spent all day Thursday trying, unsuccessfully, to figure out a way to get in touch with him. Realizing she was glancing nervously at the entrance to the restaurant every minute or so, expecting Anne Quinn or Chief Marcus to appear, Emma skipped dessert and hurried over to the cash register to pay her bill.

Retreating to her room above the Black Frog, Emma turned out the lights, climbed into bed, and realized she was going to have to find a place to hide from Anne Quinn and her questions. Listening to the murmur of voices and occasional laughter drifting up from the restaurant dock and watching the reflection of light off the lake making patterns on the ceiling, she drifted off to sleep.

Shortly after two in the morning Emma woke up. It was quiet now – the restaurant had closed and the tiki bar on the dock had shut down hours ago. She wasn't sure what had woken her – maybe a sound in the hallway. Moving to the door to her room she turned on the light and noticed a square ivory colored envelope on the floor –

apparently pushed under the door while she slept. Reaching down and picking it up, Emma noticed it was high quality and unsealed, and had her name written on the front in calligraphy. Lifting the flap she extracted a thick card and drew in a quick breath as she read its message, written in a beautiful calligraphy script.

You are invited to the wedding ceremony of
Emma L. Lange
And
Jimmy Bob Lentz
Saturday Next at 2 PM
The summit of Mount Kineo
R.S.V.P.

Emma read the invitation over again, and then turned it over. On the back was written, in block letters, "I need you to tell my story" and an email address. She turned her attention to the envelope. Reaching inside, she pulled out a small piece of threadbare blue ribbon – it was something old, something blue, and something he was letting her borrow for the wedding – all she needed now was something new.

Excited now, Emma emailed off to the address on the invitation that she very much wanted to tell the Cowboy's story and would meet him at the top of Mount Kineo the following day at the appointed time. Quickly packing her clothes she slipped out of her room and into the darkness. It was only a short walk through the small park dedicated to Henry David Thoreau to reach her car, which was parked in the large public lot next to the Moosehead Maritime Museum. Throwing her bag in the back seat Emma turned left out of the lot and headed up the east side of Moosehead Lake on Lily Bay road. About halfway to Kokadjo she made another left and drove down a steep side road toward the lake. Rounding a corner, the lakeside cabin where she had spent so many weekends as a girl came into view. It was closed up now - her good friend Jacqueline

Hollister's parents had passed away several years ago, and Jacqueline rarely visited it since moving out of state. The key to the cabin was still hidden where Emma remembered – hanging from a hook behind the "Beware of Dog" sign. Ignoring the dusty surfaces and mouse droppings, she opened several windows and flipped the main circuit breaker. Emma was sure that Jacqueline wouldn't mind her staying at the cabin for a week or so. Tomorrow she could interview the Cowboy and then hole up here at Jacqueline's cabin to write up her piece. It would be a blockbuster she was sure, and the Boston Globe would jump at the chance to publish it. Maybe she could turn it into a book. She was even willing to participate in his weird marriage ceremony if it was the price to pay for the interview, although there was no way she was going to go through with any consummation of the marriage with him. Emma had a history of taking risks and striding headlong into sketchy situations, and had convinced herself that although he had threatened his previous "brides" he had never actually hurt them much, other than the sex, and she could talk him out of the need to "put the baby."

Emma knew she had to stay off the roads – the Greenville police and county sheriff's deputies would be watching for her car now. There was another way for her to reach Mt. Kineo, however – the steamboat Katahdin would be departing on a Kineo cruise in the morning at nine AM. She was confident that she could paddle her kayak down the east side of Moosehead Lake to Greenville in the morning and slip aboard the Katahdin without being noticed. Emma and Jacqueline had often made the same trip down to the Black Frog for lunch when they had stayed at the cabin years ago.

It was clear the next morning, with a wind out of the northwest, and Emma made good time paddling down to Greenville. She stashed her kayak up against the back wall of the Kamp Kamp store, bought her Katahdin cruise ticket in the Moosehead Maritime Museum, and then sat on a bench in the deep shade until people started boarding the Katahdin for its nine o'clock cruise up to Mt. Kineo. It was scheduled to dock at Kineo at about 11:30, which would give her plenty of time for the hike to the top of Mt. Kineo and her two PM meeting with the Cowboy. Finding a spot on the upper deck with a good view of the gangway, Emma watched for familiar faces as people boarded. Once the gangplank had been hoisted onboard and Emma was confident that she hadn't been followed, she turned to look for the galley – she was looking forward to a sandwich and a strong cup of coffee. Fred Williams was leaning against the wall of the ship's cabin about 20 feet away, smiling at her.

"Glad I finally caught up with you Emma. You haven't been returning my calls."

Emma tried to rush past him but he stepped in front of her. He grasped her arm and was close enough for her to smell his aftershave.

"Emma – there's no need for concern. I'm on your side. Let me buy you something from the galley and we can sit down and talk. There's no way you can get off the Katahdin now for several hours and you don't want to make any sort of a scene and draw attention to yourself. A lot of people are looking for you right now. You don't want me to make a call do you? There's plenty of time for them to have a welcoming party waiting for you when we dock if I do."

Williams led her to a vacant table near the galley and soon returned with sandwiches and coffee. Sitting down across from Emma, he asked his first question.

"So, Emma, how's the investigation of the axe murders going?"

"Actually Fred, I've set it aside for right now – I'm looking into another interesting case – a series of rapes."

"Rapes? What are you thinking? You need to focus on the murders and making a good case that they weren't related to the Lily Bay development project."

"Sorry Fred. This rape story has better legs than the murders – and I've got a really promising angle working right now."

Williams reached across the table and grabbed Emma's wrist in a crushing grip.

"What did you and Virginia Breen's brother talk about outside the Sebec Reading Room? Did he know why his sister was killed?"

Jerking her hand away and sitting back in her chair, Emma snapped back.

"Actually, Fred, no. He would only say that she was getting involved with some shifty people and that he had left the company specifically so he would not have any involvement, and that he deliberately avoided learning anything about it. He strongly urged me to also stop poking around and to keep him out of any of my reporting."

Williams leaned back, took a sip of his coffee, and frowned at Emma.

"I'm disappointed in you Emma. You had such a bright future. Now you're off on some wild goose chase."

"Oh, I don't think so. I'm on my way to get the life story of a serial rapist who I think has quite a story to tell – a pretty strange guy who likes to marry his rape victims."

Reaching into her purse, Emma extracted the wedding invitation and handed it across the table to Williams. He read it, turned it over and read the back, and looked at Emma with an incredulous expression.

"You're not really going to meet this guy? Are you insane?"

"It's going to be fine. He never hurts his victims, other than the sex. I can humor him with a bogus wedding, get his story, and skip the sex. It's not like he will have me tied up where nobody can see me or hear me – this will be out in the open. Plus he wants his story told so he's not going to attack me."

"Emma – this is not a good idea. It's not safe. You have no idea what this guy is capable of."

Emma looked calmly across the table and responded, ending the conversation.

"Go fuck yourself Fred."

Disgusted now, Williams got up from the table and walked away.

Emma spent the rest of the cruise up to Kineo jotting down the questions she wanted to ask the Cowboy, and what she would say to distract him from any effort he might make to "put the baby."

Storm clouds were building to the north when the Katahdin moored at the Kineo dock and Emma disembarked. She remembered the rough water and heavy rain she had paddled through on her last visit to Mt. Kineo and hoped it wasn't going to be another gray and nasty afternoon. Gazing up at Mount Kineo, now looming over her, she was glad she still had almost 90 minutes to make the climb.

Somewhat resembling a slice of cake laid on its side and oriented northwest to southeast, Mt Kineo slopes gradually up to its summit from the northwest, with its southern and eastern sides formed by sheer 800-foot cliffs dropping to the lake below. Given the possibility of rough weather and strong winds that can accompany afternoon thunderstorms, Emma decided against trying the Indian Trail, which was the shortest way to the summit but required a fairly steep climb up along the southern cliff face of exposed rhyolite. Instead she took the Carriage Trail along the west shore until it connected with the gradually uphill Bridle Trail leading to the summit. The temperature steadily dropped during her leisurely hike and the few hikers coming the other way, down from the summit, gave her puzzled looks. Climbing to the top of Mt. Kineo in a thunderstorm didn't seem to them to be a very good idea. Emma just smiled and kept walking. By the time she reached the summit and the old fire tower that now served as a viewing platform for spectacular views out over Moosehead Lake, she appeared to be completely alone. A light rain had started falling, and the wind was picking up as dark clouds rolled over the summit. Emma could see no sign of Cowboy and wondered if she had been stood up. Taking shelter in a campsite lean-to close to the base of the fire tower, she checked her watch – just shy of two PM.

20
COWBOY
FRIDAY – SATURDAY

Cowboy was surprised at how easy it was to abduct George Peebles. Working from the email that had identified his final target in Maine, Cowboy researched him online and quickly planned his attack. Peebles's Facebook page mentioned his plans to go fly fishing Friday at the East Outlet of the Kennebec River with his friend Bob Whallon. A search on Google yielded numerous photos of both Peebles and Whallon, and it was a simple matter for Cowboy to find a good vantage point from which to monitor the East Outlet parking lot and wait for them to arrive on Friday morning. He watched them pull into the parking lot, change into their waders, and enter the swiftly flowing Kennebec. Smiling in anticipation as he saw Whallon moving downstream out of sight, Cowboy pulled his blue Ford pickup right up next to their car. Walking over to the river's edge, he called to Peebles, waving him over to the shore. Checking to make sure that Whallon was still out of sight downstream, Cowboy asked Peebles when he got close enough if he had jumper cables – the battery was dead in his truck.

Peebles frowned, grumbled a bit, but emerged from the river and walked over toward the two vehicles. As soon as they entered a small clump of trees Cowboy used the butt of his knife handle to knock Peebles down with a blow to the back of the head. Ripping the fly rod out of the downed man's hands, Cowboy threw it in a small ditch and pulled Peebles's hands behind his back and bound them with a zip tie. Telling Peebles to shut up as he tried to talk, Cowboy dragged him over to the Ford and pushed him into the bed of the pickup. Securing his feet with another zip tie and taping his mouth, Cowboy quickly covered him with a tarp and told him to lie still and he wouldn't be hurt. Exiting the parking lot and turning south on Route 6, back toward his barn hideaway, Cowboy didn't see the gaping pothole on the bridge, nor did he notice the axe bouncing out of the back of the truck.

The small branches he always placed across the drive leading to his hideout were still intact, indicating that nobody had been poking around during his absence. Just as Cowboy parked the Ford pickup in the barn next to the Chick Magnet and the white pickup his phone vibrated, indicating an incoming text message. Checking his phone, he was surprised by the text – "444." It was an emergency directive from his employer to vacate his location, wherever it was, immediately. He knew that Peebles was his final assignment in Maine, and he was planning on shutting down his operation and heading out in the next few days, but this was something different – the "444" message indicated an immediate threat and an urgent need for him to abandon his location as quickly as possible. He had only received the "444" warning once before, when a suspicious neighbor during an assignment in Seattle had alerted police and their raid of his hideout missed him by only a few hours.

Cowboy always prepared carefully for the possibility that he might have to break camp quickly and knew he could leave the barn behind in under twenty minutes. The first thing he should do was to tie Peebles to a tree and kill him in the manner dictated in the instructions he had received. But he had his own plans for Peebles and needed him alive for another day – just long enough to conduct a marriage ceremony. Moving his captive over to the RV, Cowboy checked his restraints and gag and locked him in the vehicle's small bathroom. The next half hour was spent checking and arming the barn's explosive devices as well as preparing the laser beam perimeter system that would set off the explosives when an intrusion occurred. Satisfied that everything was in order and that a nice surprise awaited the authorities when they converged on his hideout, Cowboy drove his Mercedes Airstream out of the barn and about 50 yards down the drive before returning to the barn to close and lock the doors. Once he reached the end of the drive he activated the perimeter intrusion system, ensuring that the barn and the vehicles inside would go up in a fireball when his pursuers tripped one of the sensors.

It was a beautiful warm sunny day in central Maine, and Cowboy was excited about being back on the road in his Mercedes and headed out of danger. By tomorrow night he will have completed his assignment, taken another bride, and be safely back over the border in Canada. He would be crossing back into Quebec at the same crossing station that he had used to enter Maine less than a month earlier, and with his Quebec license plates and driver's license and his Canadian passport, he anticipated an easy time at the border. Turning north on Route 6, Cowboy had almost reached Greenville when several police vehicles passed him going south at a high rate of speed with their light bars lit up but with no sirens – no doubt part of the posse that was converging on his hideout.

It was crowded at the Indian Hill Trading Post when Cowboy stopped for groceries, which wasn't surprising – weekenders were arriving at Moosehead on a Friday afternoon and stocking up. Feeling in the mood for a little celebration he stopped at the Dairy Bar in Greenville for a large soft serve ice cream cone. Looking across the street at the Black Frog restaurant, he wondered if Emma Lange was in her rented room preparing for tomorrow's wedding celebration.

It was only a half hour drive from Greenville up the west side of Moosehead Lake to Rockwood, where Cowboy could catch the shuttle boat over to the Kineo Peninsula. He slowed but didn't stop when he passed the Kennebec River parking lot, surprised at the large collection of people who had assembled to help with the search for George Peebles, who was safely tied up in the bathroom of his RV. When he reached Rockwood and the parking lot for the Kineo boat he pulled the Mercedes into a place at the far end of the lot, away from the other cars. After checking on Peebles – making sure he was securely tied and gagged, Cowboy locked the RV and walked over to the boat dock, joining a group of a dozen or so hikers and golfers waiting for the shuttle. He had done considerable web research on the peninsula and the different trails up to the summit of Mt. Kineo but wanted to gain first-hand knowledge of the terrain before tomorrow's marriage. He also needed to pre-position his matrimonial tool kit and a few other items he would be using tomorrow in a well-hidden but easily accessible summit location.

Cowboy took the steep Indian Trail up, lagging behind a large group of boy scouts, and found a good place to hide his backpack, slipping it under the floor of the overnight camping lean-to. His leg had been bothering him a bit recently, probably from lifting Peebles into the bed of the pickup truck, so he decided not to follow the boy scouts as they clambered up the Mt. Kineo summit fire tower. On the descent Cowboy took the Bridle Trail down the gently sloping incline to the northern tip of the island, then circled back south along the western shore, arriving at the boat dock just in time to catch the shuttle back to the mainland.

Humming to himself as he crossed the parking lot, he was disconcerted to see a young man in a game warden's uniform walking around the Mercedes and trying to peek in the windows. Cowboy called out a greeting.

"Hello. Can I help you?"

"This your vehicle?"

"Yes it is officer. Is there a problem?"

Frowning, the game warden responded.

"I'm not sure. Is there someone in there? I heard a banging noise when I walked by just now."

"Oh. That's just my dog Zack. I penned him up in the bathroom when I went over to Mt. Kineo."

Noticing the skeptical look on the game warden's face, Cowboy decided he better play it safe. No reason to get lazy this close to the end of his assignment.

"Come on in and meet Zack – he's an old dog but very friendly."

Opening the door of the RV, Cowboy ushered the game warden in and led him over to the door to the bathroom. Unlocking and opening the bathroom door, Cowboy took advantage of the warden's shock at seeing Peebles lying on the floor, bound and gagged, and pushed him violently into the shower stall. Drawing his Ka-Bar knife from its sheath he drove it into the warden's back in three swift strokes and pushed him to the floor of the shower.

Turning his gaze to Peebles, who was wide-eyed now with fear, Cowboy told him that it was his fault that the game warden was dead – if only he had stayed quiet. Watching the mortally wounded man bleed out in the shower, Cowboy had an idea. Closing the bathroom door, he got behind the wheel and headed back down Route 6 toward the East Outlet of the Kennebec River. The parking lot was empty when he arrived – apparently the search for the missing man had been called off for the day, as daylight was rapidly fading. The dead man in the shower had bled out by this time and Cowboy had a relatively easy time removing his clothes. Peebles meekly followed Cowboy's directions in shedding his own clothes and then putting on the threadbare coveralls that Cowboy pulled out of his closet. Cowboy then retied and gagged him. It was then a simple matter for Cowboy to dress the warden in Peebles's clothes and waders, smash in his face to make identification difficult, and slide his body into the Kennebec River. With any luck the body would be recovered downstream in the next day or so and would be assumed to be Peebles, further confusing the authorities, for a time at least.

Not wanting to return to the Kineo boat dock in case someone was looking for the game warden, Cowboy pulled the Mercedes into an unused campsite south of Rockwood and well off Route 6 and parked for the night. After cleaning the blood from the shower stall and feeding Peebles, he started a campfire and burned the warden's uniform. He then grilled several bratwursts over the campfire for dinner and settled in for a quiet night in front of the TV.

The next morning Cowboy was up early. He showered, shaved,

and selected a clean shirt and trousers that he thought were appropriate for an outdoor wedding. It was now just a matter of waiting for the morning to pass and making it up Mt. Kineo with Peebles in time for the two PM wedding ceremony. He wished the Patriarch and all the members of the Waldo Christian Family could be there to help celebrate his marriage to Emma Lange. He was sure they would approve. After checking on Peebles and untying him long enough to allow him to use the bathroom, Cowboy secured him again in the bathroom and sat down to make the key final instrument for his Maine marriage cluster. With tin snips, pliers, and a soldering iron he crafted an "11" branding iron in just a few minutes and tested it several times on a scrap of rawhide that already carried many of the brands that he had burned into the haunches of earlier brides. He thought of Anne Quinn as he fashioned the branding iron. He had hoped that she would be bride number eleven and had made a branding iron for her, but had dropped it into the lake after narrowly eluding capture when his B&E at her cabin had gone wrong. Cowboy didn't like leaving Maine without having the chance to make Anne his bride, but realized that they were getting closer to him now, and he had better finish up and head north.

Peebles had become increasingly agitated and frightened overnight and was more than willing to listen to Cowboy's instructions, nodding agreement and visibly trembling as Cowboy reminded him of the game warden's fate and how easy it would be to kill him in the same way if he deviated from what he was told to do. He would be untied, his gag removed, and they would ride the shuttle over to Kineo together. They would climb Mt. Kineo, Peebles would conduct the marriage ceremony, and then he would be tied to the fire tower scaffolding and left to be rescued by the next tourist to happen by. It shouldn't take too long, Cowboy assured him, and Peebles would be back safe and sound in his own bed that night. Any trouble however, any outburst from Peebles, and Cowboy wouldn't hesitate to stab him to death. Cowboy could tell that Peebles believed him and would follow instructions in the vain hope that he would be left alive after he conducted the ceremony.

The trip over to Kineo on the shuttle went without incident. Peebles was understandably subdued and clearly frightened. He thought about jumping out of the boat to escape Cowboy, but he couldn't swim that well and Cowboy sat very close and held onto his arm while keeping his other hand firmly on the handle of the Ka-Bar sheathed on his belt. They separated from the other passengers as soon as they docked at Kineo, and walking together across the golf course could easily have been mistaken for two close friends out for a leisurely stroll. Cowboy decided to not take either the gradually sloping Bridle Trail or the Indian Trail up the cliff edge, past the extensive debitage scatters resulting from thousands of years of Native American mining of the massive rhyolite deposits of the Mt. Kineo cliff face. Instead he led Peebles off the Carriage trail before they reached the Bridle Trail and they made their way up the west side of Mt. Kineo through the unmarked forest. It wasn't a difficult climb, and in spite of a nagging ache in his leg, Cowboy thoroughly enjoyed himself – the sky was darkening, the wind was picking up, and a storm was clearly on the horizon. But his upcoming nuptials put him in an upbeat mood. Life was good.

Just short of the summit Cowboy gagged Peebles and tied him to a tree before advancing carefully uphill, looking for any indication that Emma might have alerted the authorities. He doubted she had – from what he had learned about her from his web searches and her published articles she was reckless and ambitious and had little realization of the danger he actually posed. Cowboy had carried out numerous reconnaissance missions during his military training and deployments, and after a slow circling of the summit was able to both locate Emma Lange close to the lean-to shelter and to establish that there was no presence of law enforcement personnel on the mountain.

Wondering briefly how Emma had arrived on Kineo – she certainly had not taken the shuttle, Cowboy retraced his steps back to where Peebles waited bound to a tree. After offering his captive a drink of water and taking one himself, he went over again, in detail, how he wanted Peebles to behave when they joined Emma on the summit. Cowboy taped his mouth again and forced the bible he had received so many years ago from the Patriarch into Peebles's still tied hands, along with the marriage vows he had composed. Looping a rope around Peebles's neck, Cowboy jerked on it and they began climbing upslope to join his bride to be.

Emma saw Cowboy emerge from the forest due west of the fire tower. He was not alone. A second man walked just behind Cowboy, with Cowboy jerking impatiently on a rope that was tied around the man's neck. Smiling broadly at Emma, Cowboy made the introductions.

"Emma, this is George Peebles. He will be officiating at the ceremony this afternoon. George, meet Emma Lange, my fiancé."

Enjoying Emma's look of surprise, Cowboy explained.

"Pretty exciting, right? We actually have a qualified parson to marry us. He's not actually a parson or priest or anything, but I did a little research on him on the web and learned that he's a real justice of the peace and can marry people – so that's good enough for me."

Emma looked at Peebles, took in the noose, the tape across his mouth, the zip ties binding his hands in front of him, the bible, the blood and bruises, and the expression of terror on his face, and stood frozen in place. Chatting excitedly, Cowboy led Peebles over to a large tree and pushed his back up against it, then secured him by circling the tree several times with the rope around his neck and drawing it tight.

"Our celebrant, Mr. Peebles, is my last piece of business here in Maine and our nuptials this afternoon will be my final marriage here as well. And what a perfect location to bring it all to a conclusion."

Cowboy turned to take in the spectacular view out over Moosehead Lake, and Emma started shuffling slowly toward the edge of the forest behind her. Noticing her movement, Cowboy quickly walked over to her and slipping his Ka-Bar combat knife from its sheath, held it up against the side of her neck.

"Don't be nervous Emma. I'm not going to hurt you. You remind me too much of Faith, a woman who loved me and took care of me. Today we're going to be married, and then we'll consummate the marriage right here in this beautiful spot, and our child will be born into the loving embrace of the Waldo Christian Family of Heaven and Earth."

Emma's knees began to buckle as Cowboy sheathed his knife and reached into his back pocket for a large zip tie, which he fastened around her wrists. Emma bent over and retched, but Cowboy didn't seem to notice as he continued.

"Well, it doesn't look like the weather is going to cooperate, so we may as well get started."

Grabbing Emma by the zip tie around her wrists, Cowboy pulled her over to the tree where Peebles was tied and ripped the tape off Peebles's mouth. He immediately started to scream hysterically, and Cowboy hit him on the side of the head with the handle of his knife, silencing him.

"Shut it Peebles, or I'll start slicing skin off you. All you have to do is read the wedding ceremony for us and you'll be finished. Is that too much to ask?"

Peebles shook his head side to side, and silently mouthed the word "no" as Cowboy placed the knife blade along his exposed neck. Cutting the zip tie around Peebles's wrists, he pulled Peebles's hands up in front of his face.

"OK. You've got the bible and the marriage vows in your hand. My bride and I are ready whenever you are."

Cowboy held up a small velvet box, opened it, and took the modest ring out, holding it up for Emma and Peebles to see. Peebles studied the marriage vows, cleared his throat, and began. It was a remarkable scene, a marriage ceremony taking place on a promontory high above the majestic white-capped waters of Moosehead Lake, with the dark roiling clouds of a thunderstorm closing overhead.

21
DOUGLAS / ANNE
SATURDAY

Chief Marcus and his volunteers continued looking for George Peebles on Saturday morning, extending the search area outward from the banks of the Kennebec River as well as downstream. Nothing turned up by noon and the effort was called off.

Doug, Anne, and Jim Torben spent Saturday morning at the courthouse in Dover-Foxcroft going over what they had learned from the still ongoing analysis of Cowboy's burned out barn, which so far was disappointing. They had been able to identify the three vehicles Cowboy had been using from the burned out shells but no other evidence of value had so far been identified. Tire tracks leading out of the driveway were being analyzed and might provide an indication of what type of vehicle Cowboy was now driving, but lab results had not yet come back.

Still unknown was the whereabouts of three people – George Peebles, Emma Lange, and the Cowboy. They had no leads regarding the location of the three central characters in their murder investigation, but there had been some progress in the case. Paul Minnis had called Doug the night before with a plausible motive for the axe killing of Virginia Breen and the abduction and likely murder of George Peebles. He suspected that the crimes were in fact linked to a major real estate development deal, but contrary to widespread speculation, he didn't think it was the Lily Bay project.

Minnis had been digging down deeper into both Peebles and Breen's business dealings, gaining access to a number of different confidential accounts, sifting through shell companies and multiple transactions. He had discovered that the two had been surreptitiously buying up a series of properties that tracked very closely with one of the routes that had been proposed for a long-debated commercial transportation corridor across central Maine – the so-called "East-West Corridor." The proposed corridor would allow truck traffic, and a possible pipeline, to carry oil and other commodities from Canada on the west, through central Maine, to ports on the Atlantic Coast. Strongly opposed by the small communities that would be directly affected by the corridor, the project had been shelved several years ago due to the firestorm of grassroots opposition. But like many such development projects, it apparently had not been abandoned, but simply put on pause while efforts continued behind the scene.

Virginia Breen and George Peebles appeared to have somehow been privy to the still simmering plans to make the corridor a reality and both had been working to acquire property along the most likely route in anticipation of a substantial payoff when the project was revived and went forward. Minnis wasn't sure if Breen and Peebles were working independently of each other or cooperating, and he hadn't found any evidence yet of how Richard Potter was involved in the scheme. While it was a breakthrough to learn the likely underlying motive for the murders - that other potential investors in the East-West Corridor were anxious to remove their competitors – Peebles and Breen, it don't help much in actually catching the killer. He was still out there and the destruction of his hideout had left nothing that indicated where he was and what he was doing.

The anonymous phone tip came into the Piscataquis Sheriff's dispatcher a little after eleven in the morning.

"Don't bother asking who this is – I'm just a concerned citizen. I know you're looking for Emma Lange, and that she knows what the Rite Aid killer looks like. The stupid woman has somehow managed to arrange a meeting with him – she thinks he wants her to tell his story. I warned her he's likely to rape and kill her instead, but she's going through with it. The meeting, their wedding, is taking place in just a few hours on the summit of Mt. Kineo. Better hurry."

The dispatcher rushed over to the conference room where Anne, Doug, and Jim were meeting and played them the recording of the incoming phone tip. Skeptical at first and not eager to be scammed into a wild goose chase, the three investigators soon realized that they could not afford to ignore the possibility that the meeting on the summit of Mt. Kineo was going to take place. There was a good possibility that they could make it up to Mt. Kineo in time and with little discussion they hurried down to the parking lot and headed north out of town in the sheriff's SUV. Chief Marcus and several police cruisers joined them when they passed through Greenville, and they called ahead to make sure the Kineo Shuttle would be waiting for them when they reached the dock in Rockwood.

Logging trucks and road construction in Guilford slowed them somewhat, but the launch over to Kineo was waiting when they arrived. The trip across to the island was rough, with strong winds, whitecaps, and building swells. A large crowd of people was waiting at the dock on Kineo, eager to catch the shuttle back to the mainland and avoid the gathering storm. Pushing through them, Doug, Anne, and the other law enforcement officers crossed the golf course and reached the base of Mt. Kineo with about 15 minutes to spare before the two o'clock nuptials.

Following the plan they had developed on the way up, Anne, Doug, and Jim started up the Indian Trail, while Chief Marcus and the other officers took the Carriage Trail up the west side of the island. They would spread out and block any escape along the gradually sloping west and north slopes of Mt. Kineo, while also moving upslope toward the summit.

The Indian Trail was steep and demanding, particularly the first half of the climb, and Anne, who was in much better shape, moved into the lead, with Doug and Jim less than a minute behind. They were still a ways below the summit when the wedding ceremony began.

The rope that was wrapped around George Peebles's neck,

binding him tightly to the tree, made it hard for him to speak in a normal voice, and it was difficult to hear him conduct the service above the sound of the wind and the rumble of thunder as lightning lit up the sky to the north and west. Cowboy none-the-less appeared very pleased with the ceremony, and cutting her wrist tie, slipped the wedding ring on the petrified Emma Lange's left ring finger at the proper moment.

Lighting struck the fire tower, bathing the summit in bright light as Cowboy embraced Emma for the married couple's first kiss at the conclusion of the ceremony. Brimming over with happiness and holding tightly to Emma with his left hand, Cowboy turned his face to the sky and acknowledged what he had decided was the divine blessing of God and the heavens for his nuptials. Smiling gratefully at Peebles, he thanked him for a wonderful service, and grasping his Ka-Bar, swung it in a graceful motion across Peebles's exposed neck, just below the rope that bound him to the tree. A pulsing arc of arterial blood pumped from Peebles's severed throat, spraying the newly married couple with a bright red blessing of blood.

Pulling Emma back away from the dying Peebles, Cowboy looped his leg behind her knees and pushed her to the ground. Pressing the bloodied blade of his knife against her throat, Cowboy knelt astride her and bending over, spoke loudly into her ear.

"You've got a choice here Emma. If you cooperate you're going to get a great story to tell, just not the one you were hoping for. Or I can slice your throat just like I did with Peebles. I'm going to put the baby now. You can write about how you had a wonderful wedding and are so looking forward to having our baby. And the brand I give you will not only be a great picture for the story, it will also guarantee your loving acceptance into the Waldo Christian Family of Heaven and Earth. Just nod your agreement Emma."

Emma nodded, keeping her eyes closed, and Cowboy began pulling her jeans down around her ankles. She struggled against him then, and he punched her twice in the face, stunning her. Cowboy took off his trousers, dropped them to the ground, and placed his Glock pistol on top of them. Returning to Emma, who was now quietly sobbing and edging away in a backward crawl, Cowboy placed the knife against her neck and proceeded to put the baby. Her hands were not bound and while Cowboy was busy on top of her she searched frantically on the ground for something to use as a weapon. When he was finished Cowboy stood over the sobbing Emma and pulled on his pants. As he finished buckling his belt he was surprised to see Anne as she reached the summit and came into view about 20 yards away, just as the first wave of heavy windblown rain swept the summit.

Seeing Anne appear like an apparition out of the downpour, Cowboy reacted quickly. Reaching down he pulled Emma roughly to her feet with one hand and picked up his Glock with the other. Jerking Emma around in front of him as a shield, Cowboy brought his pistol up and fired at Anne, whose gun was already up and pointed at them. Anne held her fire because of the danger of hitting Emma, and Cowboy's shot was off as Emma tried to twist away from his grasp. It hit Anne in the right arm. Dropping her weapon, Anne spun sideways from the impact of the shot and stumbled close to the edge of the cliff before grabbing a tree with her good hand. Cowboy steadied for a second shot at Anne, which went wide as Emma struck at him with a rhyolite fragment she had managed to locate on the ground while she was being raped. It was a long narrow dagger-like piece of stone with sharp cutting edges that had been discarded by a Native American flint knapper thousands of years earlier. Emma swung wildly, with uncontrolled rage, at Cowboy's head, and the rhyolite dagger struck home – piercing his left eye and going through the eye socket into Cowboy's brain.

Letting go of Emma and dropping his pistol, Cowboy brought his hands up to his face and tried to extract the dagger, but it had wedged firmly in his eye socket. Covering his face with both hands and moaning, Cowboy ran blindly in a small circle several times before seeing Anne with his good eye and charging toward her, screaming in pain and rage. She pushed at him with her good arm when he came within reach and he veered off toward the cliff edge. Realizing his mistake too late, Cowboy slipped off the cliff edge into thin air and disappeared into the intensifying thunderstorm.

EPILOGUE
ONE MONTH LATER

Doug Bateman was surprised and pleased to find a parking place right in front of the Black Frog Restaurant. It was just before noon on a bright summer day and Greenville was jammed with Massholes and other tourists – lining up for soft serve ice cream and crowding into Kamp Kamp, Northwoods Outfitters, Black Frog, and the other businesses in the downtown area.

He had called Emma Lange earlier in the week and asked to have lunch with her so they could tie up some loose ends on the Cowboy case, as it was now being referred to in the press. Emma sounded enthusiastic and readily agreed to the lunch proposal. She seemed to have recovered quickly from her ordeal, with the sensation her follow-up story on the Cowboy and the Mt. Kineo marriage ceremony had created no doubt helping to lift her spirits.

Walking down the long hallway to the Black Frog Restaurant, Doug paused, as he usually did, to look at the vintage photographs of the heyday of the timbering industry that lined the walls. Two photographs of groups of loggers drew his particular attention, and he marveled again at the fortitude and determination of the lumbermen of long ago who labored through the long brutal winters of Maine.

He found Emma sitting at the bar, sipping on a cup of tea and chatting with Mitch Wagner, the owner of the Black Frog. Mitch was tall, lanky, with a full head of gray hair and large hands. He had run the Black Frog for several decades and always seemed in an upbeat mood. Today, however, he looked unusually somber and was wearing a black armband. Doug sat down next to Emma, placed a pile of folders on the bar, smiled at Emma and Mitch, and ordered a beer. As Mitch put the beer on the bar he asked the same question Doug had been hearing again and again over the past month.

"How's Anne?"

"She's doing really well, thanks to Emma here. Cowboy would have killed her up on Kineo if it hadn't been for Emma. Anne told me that Emma twisted in Cowboy's chokehold and threw off his first shot. And of course her stone dagger in the eye finished him off before he could get off a second shot."

Changing subjects, Doug asked about the armband and offered condolences. Emma burst out laughing and Mitch explained why.

"Oh, nobody died Doug, at least nobody worth mourning. That Cowboy character isn't worth even thinking about. No, I'm in mourning for the Black Frog. I've up and sold it – end of the summer, it's shutting down for good. After thirty years of slingin Cheesy Weasels, me and the wife are sellin out and heading south for the winters."

"I'm sorry to hear that Mitch – is it going to stay a restaurant?"

"That's what I hear – somebody's got fancy plans for it I think, but who knows what will happen. You know what they say – 'Maine - Where dreams come to die.'

Anyway, what other news do you have Doug? Did they find the killer's body yet?"

"Not yet. Looks like he had a clear fall 800 feet to the water. Given the wound he sustained, and the fall itself, there's little chance he could have survived. He was likely dead when he hit the water, or soon after."

Emma had been looking forward to pumping Doug about any new developments in the case, and broke in.

"What about the RV in the parking lot? Anything new there?"

"No. That was a total fuckup. We had warned everyone to stay away from it until we could bring some explosives people up from Augusta, but a couple of eager deputies apparently didn't get the message and tried to pry open the RV's door. The good news is they survived, but both received severe burns when the RV ignited. Fortunately we were able to clear the parking lot and the only other casualties were the half dozen parked cars that went up in flames. The RV and its contents were pretty much completely destroyed. There's nothing to follow up on from that angle. We were able to trace the Mercedes back to a bogus registration in Quebec, and the vehicle itself was originally sold to a shell company that has since ceased to exist. So I doubt we will ever learn who was behind the Cowboy's central Maine rape and murder spree."

Turning back to Mitch, Doug changed the subject again.

"Mitch. I'm buying Emma lunch to thank her for her courage up on Mt. Kineo, and I think we'll take a table out on the dock. I probably should take this chance to order a Cheesy Weasel and Curley Fries before the curtain falls on this place. And a draft beer for me."

Emma ordered the same and they walked out onto the deck and managed to find a table among the overflow lunch crowd. Clearly curious, Emma gestured at the folders Doug had carried to the table.

"What's with all the folders Doug?"

Doug smiled and avoided her question.

"First Emma, I want to thank you again, really seriously thank you, for what you did up on Mt. Kineo. There's no doubt Cowboy would have killed Anne if you hadn't taken him out. For that she and I will forever be in your debt. Thank you Emma."

Emma teared up, smiled, and looked embarrassed at Doug's praise. Doug continued.

"The other reason I invited you to lunch is to see what you think of a pretty bizarre theory I have been playing with regarding the Richard Potter killing. I thought that given all your research on the crime you might be willing to let me bounce my theory off you and see what you think. Keep in mind, Emma, that it's all speculative and we don't have enough evidence to pursue it any further. I've already run it by the prosecutor's office and they pretty much laughed me out the door. "

Emma's smile broadened and she replied enthusiastically.

"Excellent Doug. I can work it into something I'm working on."

"No, you won't want to do that. This is strictly deepest background – just between you and me."

Emma reluctantly took her recording phone off the table and sat back to listen to what Doug had to say. The waitress appeared just then with their burgers and fries, and when she had left Doug began to lay out his theory.

"The Potter killing has puzzled me almost from the beginning. We know Cowboy killed Peebles – you saw it up close, and we're confident he killed both O'Connell in the Rite Aid parking lot and Virginia Breen behind the Kokadjo billboard. But what if someone else killed Potter and then Cowboy decided to copy the murder in order to fit a narrative - that all three killings were by the same person and all were linked to the Lily Bay project? It would have been a brilliant misdirection on his part. Remember that we never did find any evidence to link Cowboy to the Potter murder. We never got any Cowboy DNA from the Potter crime scene. And then the axes were different – the ones used on Potter were from the Lumberman's museum and were vintage – dating to the 1940s and part of a government purchase. Cowboy's axes, on the other hand were both bought at Kamp Kamp. So why was one set of axes stolen from a museum and the other purchased from a store? Was there something special or unique about the Lumbering Museum axes? Maybe their time period of manufacture or who they were made for?"

Listening closely to Doug's theory, Emma nodded in agreement. "Sounds plausible so far."

Doug looked at his notes and continued.

"In addition, while we have continued to get new information that confirms Breen and Peebles's efforts to acquire land parcels in the path of the planned East-West Corridor and can trace their finances back to the same overseas matrix of shell companies and shady banks, Potter does not appear to have had any involvement in their scheme. So it appears likely that Potter's killer must have had a different motive."

Emma nodded again. "That sounds logical."

Doug continued.

"We've looked at all the obvious suspects – the ex-wife, the mobsters out of Boston, all the people he screwed in business over the decades, and they all came up clean as far as we can tell. So that brings me to the theory Anne and I have been working on for a while – the 'What if Emma killed Litte Rick theory?'"

Doug paused and waited for a reaction from Emma, who laughed and replied, eyes flashing.

"Now your story is getting interesting. But the prosecutor didn't think much of it?"

"No – he said I didn't have any real evidence, just conjecture, and that any decent defense attorney would laugh us out of court."

"Well then, please continue," responded Emma, leaning back in her seat and visibly relaxing.

"Emma Lange was high on our initial list of suspects, given the fact that you were the last person to see Potter alive. But we ruled you out early in our investigation. Your fingerprints were all over the crime scene, but of course not anywhere that was incriminating – not on the body or the murder weapons, or his clothes, or the rope that was used to bind him to the tree. We also looked at your kayak, and couldn't find anything there to link you to the murder. You placed yourself at the murder scene, but no one actually saw you commit the murder, and your timeline of what occurred that Sunday could be corroborated."

Emma responded.

"So no physical evidence tying me to the murder from the crime scene."

Doug nodded.

"And then there was the question of motive – what possible reason could you have had for killing Potter? You'd just met him the day before and had no prior business or personal connection to him that we could find. Maybe you two had a spur of the moment argument over your Sunday lunch and you ended up killing him. But that doesn't work since the crime was clearly premeditated. The murder weapons were stolen long before the day of the murder. Whoever killed Potter was prepared beforehand."

Doug paused to sip his beer as Emma summarized.

"So no physical evidence linking me to the murder, and no motive."

Doug nodded.

"Anne and I decided to look harder at any potential motive you might have had for killing Potter, and that led to us looking deeper into your background. I remembered then that you had mentioned in your first interview that you had a family history here in central Maine. But when I looked I found that your parents didn't immigrate to the US until the middle fifties and even then they settled in Portland, not Piscataquis County. So there didn't appear to be any Lange family history going back before the mid-fifties on this side of the Atlantic, and there was no record at all of the Langes ever spending any time in central Maine.

But then the vintage photos in the hallway here at the Black Frog, the ones documenting the history of the local lumbering industry, offered a lead. I noticed several photos they had of the Prisoner of War camp that existed during WWII up at Seboomook at the north end of Moosehead Lake. I wondered if maybe the axes from the lumberman's museum were specifically stolen because they were from the period of WWII and had been made for the US government? Maybe they were linked to the Seeboomook prisoner of war camp and something that occurred there seventy years ago. Then one evening when we're sitting on the dock and trying to see if we could cast you in the role of murderer, Anne jokingly pointed out that Lange was a German name – maybe the local family history you mentioned referred in fact to one of your ancestors having spent some time at Seeboomook during the war. That sent me back to the photos in the hallway here in the Black Frog because I remembered a group photo of some of the guards and prisoners that was taken at the prisoner of war camp. The photo included a dozen men, and all their names had been written out in a caption at the bottom. One of the prisoners shown was named Peter Lange."

Emma nodded wistfully.

"That was my grandfather. He never made it home."

"Your grandfather wasn't the only interesting individual I saw in the photo. Mitch came up behind me when I was looking at the Seeboomook group shot and pointed out another man standing off to the side holding a shotgun – obviously one of the guards. He told me that it was Richard Potter's grandfather. I looked at the name at the bottom of the picture and the man was identified as Albert Gremill, not Potter, but Mitch explained that Richard Potter was named for his adoptive grandparents, and that his biological grandfather on his father's side was named Albert Gremill."

Doug paused and Emma folded her arms across her chest and said nothing.

"That's quite a coincidence, wouldn't you say Emma – your grandfather and Richard Potter's grandfather were both in the Seeboomook camp at the same time."

"That is a surprise Doug. I had no idea."

"Anyway, to continue with our crazy theory, I got access to the negative of the photo that showed the two grandfathers from the Army Archives and had it enlarged. It showed that your grandfather was wearing a small disk on a chain around his neck with a funny squiggle on it. Curiously enough, I found more recent photos of Richard Potter's father Percy and in several of them he was wearing his watch fob with all those ornaments. One of the ornaments was a round disk about the same size as the one your grandfather was wearing in the earlier prisoner camp photo, and it seemed to have the same squiggle. Then the same watch fob, with the same disk, shows up in photos of Richard Potter, including the one you took here at the Black Frog when you had dinner with him, squiggle and all."

Stone faced now, Emma sarcastically commented.

"Wow. I agree with you Doug. You and Anne have cooked up quite a bizarre scenario. And Cannabis is not even legal yet in Maine."

Doug sorted through the top folder on the table and slid a photo across the table to Emma.

"Oh, it gets even more bizarre. I wondered what kind of disk would a German prisoner of war wear around his neck like that? It didn't take long to find a likely answer – the lightning bolt squiggle was used a lot by German youth groups in recognizing accomplishments, so your grandfather probably earned it well before he joined the military. Clearly he was proud of it."

Emma uncrossed her arms.

"I'll have to look it up. I didn't know that about grandpa Peter."

"But why then," Doug continued, "did Peter Lange's lightning bolt disk end up with Albert Gremill, who then passed it on to his son Percy and then on to Richard? Maybe he lost it in a bet or to pay a debt. This is where old newspaper articles and some oral history comes into play. The library in Dover-Foxcroft had old newspapers on microfilm, and the historical society had some audio recordings of old-timers, including Jim Asch, who actually worked as a guard at Seeboomook. I found several Bangor newspaper articles from 1944 that mentioned one of the prisoners of war escaping and then being tracked down and unfortunately killed by guards a few days later. The story stated that he attacked the guards chasing him, and they acted in self-defense. Asch, however, tells a different story. He claims in the recording he made that several of the guards, including Albert Gremill, bragged afterward about how they killed Peter Lange in cold blood and laughed about it."

Doug closed up the folder on the table and asked Emma what she thought of the theory.

"A fascinating theory Doug. Let's see if I have this right. In a nutshell, I killed Potter in revenge because his grandfather murdered my grandfather here at Moosehead Lake over seventy years ago. The problem you have, of course, is proving your theory in a court of law. You don't have any physical evidence tying me to either the murder or the theft of the murder weapons. You also can't show that Albert Gremill deliberately killed my grandfather – all you have is the hearsay statement that an addled old man heard something Albert bragged about all those years ago – not exactly admissible evidence. In addition, this disk you mentioned – my grandfather had one at the camp, and then Percy, Albert's son, shows up with one like it years later. Is it the same disk, or did he get it from a different source? If Percy did get it from his father, and his father got it in turn from my grandfather, maybe he received it as a gesture of friendship, or in exchange for extra food, or as a gambling debt. So even if the disk Percy and then Richard Potter had on their watch fobs originated with my grandfather, it certainly doesn't indicate, or even suggest, that my grandfather was deliberately murdered by Richard Potter's grandfather. You've got nothing."

Nodding in agreement, Doug responded.

"That's pretty much what the prosecutor said – intriguing theory that lacks enough evidence to proceed unless you can get a confession."

"No chance of a confession from me Doug. Not a chance."

"I didn't really expect you to confess Emma. Why would you, in the absence of any real proof? Maybe we would have a better case if we ever were able to find the disk – it looks like whoever killed Potter also stole the disk from him. We recovered the watch fob along with the second axe stolen from the lumbering museum – the one used to cut his spinal column in half, in the water off his dock, and the disk was one of two ornaments that had been removed. If the disk does ever turn up, and I doubt it will, whoever ends up having it in their possession would have some explaining to do."

Emma said nothing and sat rock still as Doug, smiling broadly now, looked pointedly at the chain around her neck. Whatever was on it was hidden underneath her sweater, and she made no movement toward showing Doug what she now carried with her wherever she went. After a long strained silence between them, Doug continued.

"Anyway, I thought I would tell you about our theory, since it might have involved your grandfather. But it's only a theory. Anne wanted me to say that she is doing really well – her arm is healing quickly, although ball handling on that side will be awkward from here on. And she sends her best. We both are so grateful for the courage you showed up at Kineo."

Doug stopped, smiled, looked up the lake at a floatplane coming into land, and asked his final question.

"Emma, how about another beer?"

ABOUT THE AUTHOR

B.D. Smith was raised in Detroit, Michigan, and attended the University of Michigan where he received his undergraduate and graduate degrees in prehistoric archaeology. Before turning to writing fiction he authored numerous scholarly books and articles on the origins of agriculture and other topics. He and his wife live in Santa Fe in the winter and spend their summers in Bowerbank, Maine.

Thank you so much for reading one of our **Crime Fiction** novels.
If you enjoyed the experience, please check out our recommended title for
your next great read!

Caught in a Web by Joseph Lewis

"This important, nail-biting crime thriller about MS-13 sets the bar very high.
One of the year's best thrillers." –*BEST THRILLERS*